ANIMOSITY

JASMIN HUDSON

DEDICATION

I dedicate this project to my lovely mother and father, there would be no me without you.

To my children: Yasmine, Jasmond, Damarion, Kemel, Antonio, and Jasmin Jr. To my grandkids: Mckenzie, Paisley, Emerald, Kaydence and Major. You all are the reason why I go so hard. You all are my reflection, my legacy. I love ya'll with all my heart.

To my ancestors for continuously watching over me and the sacrifices they made in order for me to become the man I am today.

To all my family and friends, thank you for believing in me and giving me the strength and encouragement that I needed at a time when I didn't believe in myself. I will forever appreciate your input.

TABLE OF CONTENTS

ACKNOWLEDGMENTS

Thank you to everyone who participated in the creation of Animosity.

Thank you to my editor , Lataryn Rainey-Perry at Penwork Publishing. You're the best and I look forward to doing more work with you.

Thank you Bert Ford, my graphic designer, for my book cover. I gave you a vision and you made it a reality.

Most of all, thank you to my family. My superwoman, my best friend, my rock, my everything, my mother Ms. Mary…love you lady. Shoutout to my hero, my mentor, my backbone, my father Mr. Marion. I have many friends who either never grew up with their fathers or never met them. I'm thankful you've been there for me.

Shoutout to my big sis, Nikki. No matter the distance between us our hearts are never far apart. Love you big sis. To my other sister, Che-Che, who calls me every day being sickening but always making sure I get a home cooked meal, thank you. I love you girl.

Special shoutout to my special friend, Aja Myers. You are the truth babe. You keep me grounded. Through my downs and ups, you stuck by my side and I appreciate you for being the person that you are. Thank you for loving my kids like your own. You already know I love Ja'Claja (Clay) and Ashanti Jr. (Phatboy) as if they were mine.

Shout to all of my nieces and nephews. They would've killed me if I didn't mention them. Ta'shanta, Dominic, Quesha, Tonjala, Monteco, Kenya, Veshia, Vashia, Jermashia, and Jylashia.

I'd also like to thank my baby mothers LaShawna, Shanicqua, Kimberly, Itesha and Aja for blessing me with the joy of life as a father. I appreciate all of you for having patience and faith in me as a father. Thank you!

Shout out to my Money $ Mount family and the whole Charleston a.k.a Chuck Town area: 10 mile, Liberty Hill, Russeldale, Furndale, Liberty Park, Tha Phate, Midland Park, Money $ Macon, Accabee, The Hike, Hub Village, The Waylon, Ashley Shores, P.C.P a.k.a The Project a.k.a Horizon Village, Strawberry Lane, Romney St. Village, Spring St., Bay Side, Back Tha Green, Wilson St., East side, Sunny Side, The B.I., Mt. P, West Ashley a.k.a West Cash, Red Top, James Island, and Johns

Island.

Shout out to my bros that were locked up with me on SMU. I appreciate all of the positive feedback and constructive criticism ya'll gave me while I was writing this book. You all were my first critics. If it weren't for me being locked in a cell 23/7 this book would've never been manifested.

Thank you Bianchi a.k.a Newton.

Last, but certainly not least, I want to say thank you to my readers.

Free: Ice'em, Pumpkin, Gee'z, Plat, T.Shine, Lil Web Cheeks, Jo Jo, Mean Man and BooBee.

Long Live: E.J, Z.B, Gully Boy, Jose, Lil Teezy, Smiley, Frost, New York Rob, Runt, Boy Boy, Twin and York.

#SomebodyGottaTellTheStory

PROLOGUE

"Man, I can't wait to get out dis hell hole they call prison," Red said to his roommate. "It's been five and a half years and it seems like time done start slowing down since I'm down to my last few months."

Red stood 5'10, weighed 170 and was stocky with brown eyes and light skin. He had eight gold teeth, four at the top and four at the bottom, and his upper body was covered with prison tattoos.

"Mane, fall back playa. You ain't got long." Cool Hand said as he shuffled the deck of cards in his hands. Cool Hand was Red's roommate. He stood at 5'8, weighed 160 lbs. and was brown skin with two open face gold teeth at the bottom of his mouth. Cool Hand was from Memphis, Tennessee, but got cased up in Columbia, South Carolina.

"Aye, real talk, I'ma mix all them so call niggas that supposed to be my friends. Every time I talk to them bitch ass niggas they feed me a bunch of bullshit like they really got my back." Red stated.

"Check it homie, you already know what that shit hittin' fo pimp, so I can't see you stressin' yo'self behind that shit." Cool Hand replied.

"I ain't stressin' zeek. I'm shittin'! If the shoe was on the other foot, them niggas know I would've played the game fair. The bad thing about it is them niggas is major."

"I pimps baby! That's all I know and that's all I'ma do when I get out this bitch." Cool Hand replied.

"Pimp on nigga, pimp on. But them niggas gonna regret the day these folks set my black ass free. Mark my words. Call me Chris Brown cause it's on and poppin'."

***

Operator: *To except this collect call from…"Red", please push zero. Please do not use three way or call waiting or this call will be disconnected. Please push zero now.*

"What's up, Red," Slim said when the line was connected.

"Ain't nothing man. I'm just right cha' chillin'." Red replied.

"It ain't long now, Lil bruh."

"And you know I can't wait."

"So, what's up? You get that bread that me and Jigga sent you?"

"Yeah, I got dat. Nice lookin' out. But check it, you be seeing Trap, G-Money, C. Lo, or Tee Tee around?"

"I be seeing them niggas when I be out and about but them niggas don't come round the Mount like that unless somebody call one of dey ass. Lil bruh, them niggas out cha' hella mixin'. Feel what I'm saying?"

"You know dem niggas shit on me right? They ain't did shit for me the whole time I been lock up. Dem supposed to be my peoples. I got a lot of anna on my chest, real talk!"

"Lil bruh, dem been your friends but fuck'em. You don't need them niggas. You know the Mount got your back. Get your weight up with your hate and pay'em back when ya bigger."

"I feel ya zeek. I like how that sounds. Tupac couldn't have said it no better. How's Tiny and my daughter doing?"

"Tiny right downtown on Johnson St. projects tryna do everybody hair and Kaela gettin' bigger and badder. Want me to call them on three way?"

"Yeah, do that for me."

"Hang up and call back so you can get the whole 15."

"Alight, bet. Aye, you know I touch down in three more months, right?"

"Yeah, I know."

"Me and you gonna pay all dem boy a visit, feel me?"

"Already. What's understood don't need to be explained. Now hang up so I

can call Tiny for you."

***

Three months later...

"Damn, these muthafuckas need to hurry up. You know I'm tired of seeing this place." Red said to Cool Hand.

"Tighten up playa. You're leaving today regardless." Cool Hand stated

"I know, I'm just ready to go now. You got my address and phone number, use that shit anytime zeek. I got you and that's my word."

"Playa, you don't owe me nothing. My hoes got me and that's law. Just stay sucka free, ya dig? I ain't got long myself. If I drop you a letter from back here, I'll just be checking on you but if I don't, I'll holla at you when I touch down."

"Make sure you holla at me for real, for real."

"Jasmond Welch! Jasmond Welch! Please report to the admin building with all your belongings!" a lady's voice yelled over the loudspeaker.

"That's me, Cool. Make sure you holla at me." Red said giving Cool Hand dap.

"Remember what I said...Stay sucka free pimp."

"Yeen know!" Red replied copying a word he always heard Cool Hand saying.

When Red stepped through the prison gates, Slim, his baby mother Lisa, Slim's son Mann and Red's girlfriend Tiny, along with their daughter Kaela, were all awaiting him.

Red got down on his knees and kiss the ground. "Free at last, free at last. Thank God almighty I'm free at last!" he yells out quoting Martin L. King.

CHAPTER 1

Slim picked up his ringing cell phone and said, "What's up?"

The person on the other end of the phone said, "What you getting into?"

"Who tha fuck this is?" Slim asked back.

"This Red, nigga. I know you got me lock in. Look at your caller I.D. zeek! Wussup wit cha?"

Slim said, "Oh...man, I'm just chillin' with the family. What's good with you?"

"I'm mackin'. I got us a lil mission set up. How u rockin'?"

"Hold up, let me get up and walk in the other room... Ok, holla at me."

"I found out where that nigga Trap lay his head at. I been

following dude for the last few days." Red told him.

"Oh word?... How his set up looking?"

"Dat nigga live up there in Dorchester Manor in a duplex apartment. It got a fence round the back yard. I used to fuck with a broad who use to live around there before I got locked up, so I know how the inside of his spot looks. The only problem is, we got to go in through the front door."

"Why the front door and not the back?"

"Cause it ain't got no back door. It got one of them sliding glass doors that's connected to the kitchen."

"When you tryna do this shit bruh?"

"Tonight!"

"Come scoop me later then."

"Say no more." Red said.

Slim hung up the phone and went back into the front room to finish looking at tv with Lisa and his son.

"I guess you're about to leave?" Lisa asked.

"Not right this minute, but I'm checking out in a few hours. Why you ask?"

"I just thought you was gonna stay in for the night."

"That was the plan, but something came up. You already know how that is."

"You right...I know how that is... just be careful."

"All the time baby. All the time."

***

"Yo Slim, I'm outside nigga." Red said when Slim answered his phone.

"I'm walking out right now." Slim step out his door wearing black cargo pants, a long sleeve black shirt, a black knitted cap, black gloves, and all black Timberlands. Red was camouflaged from head to toe. He even had a camouflage bandanna tied around his neck.

"You ready?" Red asked.

"Ain't I in the damn car nigga? Let's ride and get this shit over with so I can get back home and fuck my gal before it gets too late."

It took them 30 minutes to get from Remount road to Dorchester Manor. They rode by Trap's spot to make sure his Chrysler 300 was there. When they saw his car, they park two duplexes down and walked back to the duplex that Trap lived in.

"How you wanna to do this?" Slim whispered.

"How you mean?" Red whispered back.

"Do you want to knock and see if he answer the door or you want to just kick this bitch in? Your call lil bruh."

"Make me no difference. Fuck it, we can do both."

"Well, knock. As soon as he say who, I'm kicking that bitch in."

***

Trap was in the process of eating pussy when he heard someone knocking on his door.

"Damn! Hold on baby, let me see who tha fuck this is knocking on my fucking door at this time of night." Trap said agitated.

"Hurry back baby." The female said in a sexy tone.

Once Trap got to the door, he looked through the peephole but couldn't see anything due to the porch lights being out. At the same time, the person on the other side of the door began knocking again. In the back of his mind, Trap knew that something wasn't right. So, he ran to the hall closet and grab his .357 and came back to the door.

"Who is it?" he asked.

Before he could react, the door smacked him in the face and his gun flew out his hand as he fell to the floor. When he looked up, two men were standing over him. One in all black with a black bandana over his face and the other in camouflage attire wearing the same printed bandana over his face.

Hearing the commotion coming from the front room, Trap's female friend peeked out the bedroom door to see what was going on. When she saw two mask men standing over Trap, she started screaming. Red left Slim with Trap as he ran to the room where she was.

"Bitch, shut the fuck up before I pop yo stupid ass!" Red said.

"Please don't hurt me!" the female replied.

"Just sit yo ass on that bed and don't say shit bitch!"

The scared female sat on the bed shaking like a leaf as she shook her head up and down to let him know she understand. Red was about to walk out the room, but he turned back around pulling a roll of duct tape out his pocket. He placed tape over her mouth, then he bound her hands behind her back. Before he taped her ankles together, he played with her pussy. Then he left her laying on the bed.

When Red walked back to the front of the apartment, Slim had

Trap sitting on the couch in his boxers with blood coming from his head. Slim was sitting across from him with his gun pointed at him.

"Tape that nigga up, but don't cover his mouth." Slim stated. After Red finished taping Trap up, Slim said, "Now Trap, we either can do this the hard way or the easy way. Fast or slow. The choice is yours, ya feel me? You know what we want and we ain't leaving until we get it."

"Ya'll lil niggas really think ya'll gonna get away with this shit?" Trap asked.

Slim looked at Red and Red pistol-whipped Trap across his face causing him to scream out in pain.

"Fuck ya'll!" Trap yelled spitting out blood and pieces of his chipped tooth.

"Oh shit, I see we got us a gangsta. So, you on that gangsta shit, huh? Let's show this bitch ass nigga what we do to gangstas. Cut that tape off his legs and take his boxers off. Let's show him who the real gangstas is."

Trap tried to put up a little struggle but Red got him out of his boxers and taped his legs back together. Then Red and Slim both carried Trap to the bedroom where his female friend was.

"Now, I'ma ask you one more time, nigga. How you wanna to

do this shit? The easy way or the hard way? Because you're wearing out my patience." Slim stated.

When the female heard Slim's voice, she started screaming something but with the tape over her mouth it was hard to make out what she was saying.

Trap spit on the floor through bloody lips and said, "Fuck ya'll!"

"That's what I'm talking about. Have it your way lil nigga." Slim said as he stood up and put his gun on his waist then walked out the room with Red right behind him.

"Nigga, what you about to do?" Red asked.

"Get a knife out the kitchen." Slim answered. "I'm about to see how long he gonna put up this gangsta act."

Red nodded. "Bring the bitch out of that nigga. I know I heard something fall on the floor when we first came in."

"I heard that shit too. Go look over there by the door."

Red searched by the door and said, "Muthafucka had a gun!"

"Watch me make this muthafucka squeal like a pig." Slim said coming out the kitchen with a steak knife.

Trap and the female's eyes grew big when they saw Slim coming back in the room with the steak knife.

"Aye, my nig. Roll something up and turn that radio on over there. Turn it up loud. Since Trap so gangsta, we gonna be here for a while. Let's get gangsta nigga." Slim said as Red turned on the radio.

As soon as Red turned the volume up, Slim stabbed Trap in his right thigh. He drove the knife so deep into Trap's leg that only the handle was visible. Trap screamed so loud that Red had to put tape back over his mouth. Slim then yanks the knife out of Trap's thigh and did the same exact thing to his left leg.

"Take that shit nigga! You're a gangsta, right? Speak up nigga, I can't hear you!" Slim teased.

Red walked out the room to finish rolling the blunt. He didn't want to take his bandana off in front of Trap and the female.

Meanwhile, back in the room, Slim was asking Trap if he was ready to talk. Trap shook his head up and down, but Slim stab him in the right thigh again for good measure. The female blacked out.

Slim ripped the tape off Trap's mouth and said, "Talk to me."

Trap was in so much pain that he barely made any sense. "D-dah...d-dope... dog-dog-doghouse...in-in-in th-the back."

Slim slap him on the thigh and Trap screamed out in pain. Slim said, "See, that wasn't so hard gangsta bitch, now was it?"

Slim placed the tape back over Trap's mouth and walked out

of the room. Him and Red went out back to check the doghouse. They were both expecting to see a dog, but to their surprise, there was none. They stood in the back yard and smoked the blunt that Red had rolled. Then they began pulling bricks of coke from out of the doghouse.

"It's my turn to apply pressure. Let's go find out where he got that check from." Red said.

"Do ya thing family. The ball is on your court."

They walked back into the apartment and headed for the room. Trip's female friend had woken back up. By the look in her eyes you could tell she was scared as hell. She was trying to say something, but it was hard to make out what she was saying through the duct tape and the radio. She kept her eyes on Slim.

This time Red was sitting in front of Trap. Red pulled Trap's .357 from his pocket and asked Trap, "What were you gonna do with this? I should kill yo' bitch ass, but I'ma give you a chance to redeem yo'self. You with that?"

Trap shook his head so hard that if it weren't for his neck, his head would've fell right off.

"Aight then, where's the money at?" Red asked as he pulled the tape from Trap's mouth.

"I swear man all I got is a couple of stacks in my pants

pocket." Trap answered.

"Wrong answer, homie." Red replied as he put the tape back over his mouth. He then took a torch lighter out his pocket. "Hold this nigga, big homie." he said to Slim.

Slim held Trap in place as Red grabbed ahold of Trap's penis. He lit the lighter and with no hesitation, he placed the torch flame on the head of Trap's penis. This time the girl broke wind and pissed on herself at the same time. Then she passed out again.

Trap's eyes and cheeks puffed out like a blow fish as his high pitch screams were muffled behind the duck. He wiggle like a fish on dry land in Slim's hands as he tried to get away from the burning sensation of the torch. Not even the duct tape could stop the animalistic moans coming from his mouth.

"Where that check at nigga? Tell me or I'm gonna burn this little shit the fuck off!" Red demanded.

"It's in the middle room. In an old black and white tv!" Trap screamed with no hesitation soon as Red snatched the tape off of his mouth.

"How much?"

"I don't know, about a buck fifty." he answered with sweat and tears pouring down his face.

Red gave Slim a head nod. Slim walked out of the room to

grab the tv from the middle room. After finding a screwdriver in the hall closet, Slim removed the screws on the tv. Just as Trap has said, the money was there. Slim closed the tv back up and screw the screws back in. He then walks over to the female and shot her two times in the chest. As if on que, Red stood up and shot Trap three times. Once in the stomach and twice in the chest. Red and Slim grabbed the four bricks of coke and the tv, then they ran out to the car they had park up the road. They headed straight back to the Mount. The entire ride was silent. Both men were wrapped up in their own thoughts.

"Slim, why you shot that broad? She ain't see us." Red asked breaking the silence.

"I used to fuck that bitch, zeek. The whole time she been screaming through that tape, she been trying to call my name. We can't afford no mistakes and I ain't trying go to jail."

"I can feel that. When I drop you off, I'm leaving all this shit with you. We can fuck with this shit tomorrow. I'm about to go lay it down for the night."

"Bet, but on the real though, I should've put that fire to ole boy ass from the go. We would've been out that mix and in tha house by now."

"I already know. The thought came to me when we was in the back yard smoking that blunt. But fuck it, we did that my nigga.

Word!"

Red dropped Slim off and went in for the rest of the night.

Back in Dorchester Manor, Trap was laying on the bed bleeding to death when a nosy neighbor walked in and said, "Is anybody in here?"

From the back room, in a faint voice, Trap says, "Please help me...I'm back here." Then he passed out.

CHAPTER 2

Lisa woke Slim up and handed him his ringing cell phone. As soon as he grabbed the phone, it stopped ringing.

"What time is it?" he asked, yarning while wiping the sleep from his eyes.

"A lil after 12 p.m. Your phone been ringing for the last 30 minutes." she responded.

"I'm surprised you ain't answer it with yo' nosy ass."

"Maybe that's because I already know who it is. That ain't nobody but Red. Oh, but best believe if I did not know the number, I would've answered it."

Slim's phone started ringing again.

"Yooo... Wussup my nigga?"

"Damn zeek! You just getting up?" Red asked.

"Yeah. Where you at lil nigga?"

"About to be pulling up in front of your yard. It's hot as a muthafucka outcha. Ball (police) everywhere! You need to move off dis hot ass Mount. Word!"

"Nigga, I ain't leaving tha Mount. You can forget dat. This my hood. Aye Lisa, open the door for Red! The door open. I'm about to brush my teeth. Holla at you when you come in." Slim hung up.

"Wussup, Red?" Lisa greets him as he enters the house.

"Ain't shit L, wussup with you? Where yo skinny ass man at?" Red asked.

"I'm just chillin'. He in the back putting his clothes on. He is coming. You want something to drink while you wait?"

"Naw, I'm good. Thanks though."

***

Slim walks into the front room about 15 minutes later and gave Red dap. "I thought you would've been come in. You made it seem like you was already in front of my house."

"Nigga, I was already on your street when I called but I kept on riding because Ball been behind me. I told you dey hot outcha.

Fuck is you bitching about anyways? I still had to wait damn near 20 minutes for you to come outcha."

"Whatever nigga! Let me get rid of Lisa, then we can handle our business...Aye Lisa!"

"What boy? Stop all that damn yelling!"

"I need the house for a few hours. Why don't you go hit the mall or something? And pick Mann up from school while you out there."

"I guess I can go get my feet and nails done. I need some change."

"I got about 400 dollars in my other pants pocket in the room. Go ahead and get that. Buy Mann some shoes too."

"Aight. Let me get myself together so I can get out of ya'll's way."

"Red, I know you got something to smoke. Roll up zeek. That'll give Lisa enough time to get the fuck on."

"You already know I keep that green on deck. But I ain't got no white." Red responds with a smile.

"Like that's really a problem. You know we got that white girl on deck."

Slim and Red sat at the kitchen table, with the TV from the

robbery open as they count the money that was inside of it. $148,000 was the total amount of money. A 50/50 split left them both with two bricks and $74,000 each.

"Man bruh, I would have never expected that check to be duck off in this old ass TV." Slim stated.

"Who you tellin'? That been a platinum spot for real. If I hadn't put that fire on his dick, we probably would've never find that money." Red said.

"Honestly, the nigga probably had more bread then that."

"Shid, if he did then that's an afterthought. I'm good with what I got out of his ass."

"Me too. I was just speaking out loud. The crazy shit is, that nigga been fuckin' a broad I use to fuck wit. A Bitch named Mcka. That bitch had to recognize my voice because I know for a fact she couldn't tell who I was by looking at me."

"Word! No wonder why she been looking at you the whole time. How come I don't know who she is?" Red asked.

"She been a lil mix I been fuckin' on the low while you was lock up."

"Well, fuck em'. She been in the wrong place at the wrong time. We need some more blunts. Let's walk to the corner store on tha 4-way."

Attaway St. and Sumner Ave. is considered to be the 4-way. That's where most of the drug dealers from the Mount sell their drugs at.

"Aight, let me go put this shit up."

"Put my stuff up for me too. Make sure you ain't dirty. I already told you Ball riding hot tonight."

"It's Thursday. You think I don't know?"

"These lil niggas outcha crazy. They don't give a fuck about nothing." Red stated as he and Slim walked down Sumner Ave. together heading for the corner store.

"Why you say that?" Slim asked.

"Because they see all these police riding round dis bitch and they still outcha posted up on the corner and running to cars like that shit legal. That's why they ass stay lock up."

"No! That's how they make their money, zeek. Damn dawg, you act like you ain't never been outcha before. Nigga, you use to hustle in front of that same corner store or has prison made you forget?" Slim asked cutting Red off.

"Ball ain't used to fuck with us like that though. Don't get me wrong, I ain't tryna knock nobody's hustle but them lil niggas just need to be smarter and move better."

"Whatever nigga. You're just seeing things through different eyes, zeek. We been hot as fuck, too. But speaking for myself, I'ma hustler so I'll come post up right on this same corner and hustle with these niggas if I have to, or I'll just come through and shoot the shit. We might not have the same motivation to our cause, but our struggle is damn near the same. You can never forget where you started at or where you come from or you'll never know where you're going. Remember that." Slim said.

"What's up Lo-Lo, Chedda, Double R., and Plat." Slim and Red said as they walk past them going in the corner store.

"Wussup Slim... Wussup Red." They all greeted back.

"You want something to drink Slim?" Red asked as he headed for the cooler in the back of the store.

"Yeah, snatch me a Red Bull."

Red nodded and said, "Bet. Grab me a pack of Newport."

While Red and Slim was standing at the counter placing their order, Chedda and Plat ran in the store and said, "Don't go out there! Ball got Lo-Lo, Double R and a couple more people hem up outside!"

"See what I told you!" Red said nervously.

"Nigga, we ain't dirty. Fuck is you nervous for? Let's ride. Plat hit me up later. I got a play in motion. Ya'll be careful outcha. I'm out."

Just as they were exiting the store, an office that everybody in the hood calls Big Face said, "What's up Red. Haven't seen you in a while. What's up Slim. Let me see some I.D.'s."

As soon as he said that Double R takes off running. Big Face and another officer takes off behind him. With that distraction Red and Slim got light.

"I'm glad Double R took off running because I damn sure didn't have my I.D on me." Red stated.

"Me neither. Muthafucka been ready to give us a ticket."

"I told you tha Mount fuck up."

"Downtown fuck up too, dawg!"

"Yeah, but Ball don't be fuckin' with a nigga like that down there. Open tha door before Ball come round this bitch looking for us."

"Come on with your scary ass! You ain't even dirty and you're actin' like a run-away slave."

"Bitch! Your ass been running too. Next time, we mixin' at my spot."

"Whatever nigga and watch ya mouth. I got yo bitch, nigga. I'm about to call Lil Reezy, Budda, and Peter Roll. I'ma throw them boy a quarter a piece for 8 stacks. When Plat call me, I'ma throw him the other quarter. So that's already one brick gone."

Slim stated.

"One of my peoples from downtown want to cop a half. That's one of the reason's I been calling you so early, but when I saw Ball round this bitch, I called dawg and told him to give me a couple of hours. Plus, Booja say he gonna get with me when he come out. I do need to call D. Money and Lil V because I been promise them boy I was gonna look out." Red said dialing a number on his cell phone.

"Well, let's hurry up and make these calls. Tell them boy to hurry up. I don't like doing this shit around Lisa and Mann. Especially lil Mann.

"Their probably on their way back now, anyway."

"Yeah. You rolling with me downtown, right?" Red asked.

"That's a major 10-4."

***

"Baby, I'm about to shoot D.T. with Red for a lil while. I'll be in early tonight." Slim tells Lisa as he heads for the door.

"A'ight, just be careful out there. The police still riding round acting crazy." she responds.

"Oh yeah, if Plat comes by tell him to hit me on the jack

(phone) cause I done been waiting on him for the longest... Come on Red, lets slide."

"I already tell you about having them hot ass niggas coming here. You ain't gonna stop until the police run up in here. If they do, you can't blame nobody but ya'self." Lisa complained.

"Girl, who the fuck is you talking to? Don't even try to handle me like that in front of Red. Plat ain't no hotter than yo punk ass cousin who be walking his hot ass round here every chance he gets. His ass stay in jail."

"Boy please! Who the fuck is Red? You know what? I ain't even about to stand here and go back and forth with you. I'll see you later!"

At this time Red was in the car laughing hard with tears coming out of his eyes.

"Fuck is so funny nigga?" Slim asked.

"You nigga! L about to whip that ass!" Red answered still laughing.

"You know that's how me and Lisa get down. Hit Remount road and go straight to the I (interstate) cause I ain't trying to get hem up bruh."

"That's the way I been going anyway."

As Red and Slim were riding down the interstate, headed for

downtown, Slim's phone started ringing.

"Yooo, who dis?"

"Dis Plat my nig. I'm walking up B. Dub (Blackwell St.) now."

"Damn zeek, I done slide. I'm on my way downtown. I tried to wait on you."

"Man, those fucking dicks had me trap off on the Bottom (Read St.). When are you coming back through? I need ya zeek! Good word."

"I ain't even gonna lie, I ain't trying see tha Mount for a lil sec. That bitch too hot. Tell you what, let me hit up Budda and tell him to give you something until I get back on the Mezzy (Mount)."

"Man, Budda be taxing." Plat complained.

"Nigga chill! Everything going through me. I'm about to call bruh right now."

"Bet it up." Plat stressed before hanging up.

"If you had brought that shit with you, he could've rode with Booja when he come to holla at me later." Red said.

"Everything good. I do my business in the North. Hold on," Slim says as Budda answers his phone. "Yo B, wussup? I need you to do me a favor."

"Wussup zeek. Holla at me." Budda responded.

"I need you to throw Plat a four deuce (ounce and a half) until I get back in the North."

"How long you talking, Slim? You know how you like to take your time to do everything."

"About two, no longer than three hours bruh."

"A'ight. Why can't I just have the sell?"

"It ain't even that type of party. Go call dawg, he's waiting on you to hit him up."

"Bet. Holla at me later." Budda hung up.

***

Turning onto Nassau street, in an area called the Johnson Street projects, one of Red peoples named Dolla was sitting on the porch in front of his apartment waiting for him.

"Wussup Bo-Lo?" Dolla greeted Red once he got out of the car.

"Wussup Dolla Bill. This my nigga Slim." Red said while grabbing the TV from the back seat of the car.

"Wussup." Slim and Dolla said greeting each other with a

head nod.

"Slim, grab these keys and catch the door for me." Red instructed.

When they walked into the house, Red went straight upstairs with the TV. His baby's mother, Tiny, was in their bedroom doing one of her friend's hair.

"Hey baby." Tiny greeted.

"Hey babe." Red responded and gave her a kiss. "Don't we have a screwdriver around here somewhere?"

"Yeah, downstairs in the kitchen draw. Why?"

Without answering her question, he went back downstairs to get it. After finding what he was looking for, Red came back upstairs and asked where Kaela was.

"She's outside on the park in the back. Why?"

"Girl, would you stop asking me questions every time I ask you a question! Damn! I need to go in her room for a minute."

"Boy please! That's all you had to say. Gosh!"

Red sucked his teeth and went into Kaela's room. "Oh yeah! I got company downstairs too!" he yells before closing the door.

"Girl, yo nigga be acting up." Tiny's friend, Boo, whispered.

"Who you telling? He just showing his ass off. He know I don't play that shit," Tiny said.

Boo sucked her teeth and they both bust out laughing.

Red stuck his head out of the door and said, "Aye babe, can you hand me my clock (scale) and my box of sandwich bags out the closet."

When Tiny brought the bags and scale into the room, her eyes grew big at the sight of all the drugs and money on the bed next to the old TV. Red stood next to the dresser breaking down dope not paying her no mind. Without saying a word, she put the bags and scale on the bed and left the room.

"Bring me some rubbing alcohol and a rag so I can wipe this dresser off when I'm done." Red called after her. He never looked up from what he was doing.

Five minutes later, Tiny brought the alcohol and rag for him. Then went back in her room to finish her friend's hair.

***

Due to the fact that Red had a little scale he had to weigh the coke in zone (ounces). So, he bag up 18 individual zones and put it to the side. Then he bag up the last 9 zones from the brick for Booja. He had to get 4 grams from the other brick to make it come out even. Earlier he fronted Lil V and D-Money a biggy (4 ½ ounces) for $4000 apiece.

When Red was done, he cleaned his mess and wiped the dresser down with the alcohol that Tiny had brought to him. He then placed everything back in the TV with the exception of the coke he'd just bag up. After putting the TV on the top shelf in Kaela's closet, he went back downstairs where Slim and Dolla were awaiting him.

"Damn Bo-Lo, I thought you done forgot we were down here." Dolla exaggerated.

"Naw nigga, I had to get this shit together. I ain't got no big scale." Red replied.

"I rolled up a couple of blunts while we been down here waiting on your slow ass." Slim stated.

"Whatever nigga. We gotta smoke this shit on the porch because Kaela lil ass is home." Red said as he handed Dolla the 18 zones and the scale. At the same time, Dolla handed him a McDonalds bag with thirteen stacks in it.

Dolla weighed the dope while Red counted the money. After everything was good, they gave each other dap and Red walked Dolla to the door.

"I'll get at you later, Bo-Lo." Dolla said then walked to his car.

"Say no more. Be easy family." Red replied. "Slim, come on out here and fire that shit up zeek."

By the time they were firing up the second blunt, Booja was pulling up.

"Man, ya'll got outcha stink with that boonk shit. Word!" Booja said when he got out his car.

Slim started laughing and asked Booja if he wanted to hit the blunt.

"Boy, I don't smoke that stink ass shit! Let me get my shit so I can slide." he shook his head. "Slim, you hell."

"Come on zeek. I got your shit ready." Red said leading Booja into the house.

Kaela was in the kitchen when Red and Booja walked into the house.

"Hey daddy!" she screamed excitedly as she rushed him, almost knocking him over, and hugged his legs.

"Hey Baby K!" he hugged her back. "Listen, run upstairs for daddy and get my car keys from your momma"

As soon as Kaela was out of sight, Red handed Booja the nine zones in a grocery bag.

"Everything good my nigga. I got that shit scaled out right. Shoot me the money before my daughter come back down."

"I respect that so I ain't gonna trip about you rushing me, but if this shit ain't on time, I'm calling you asap. I'm out." Booja said walking to the door.

"Momma say her don't know where your keys at." Kaela said running pass Booja.

"Thank you, baby. I thought she had them but they were in my pocket the whole time. Go on back outside to the park and be careful out there."

"Yes sir." Kaela ran off.

"Nigga, this check better be right or I'ma short yo ass for sure next time." Red joked as he walked Booja out the door.

"My check always on time zeek. I'll holla at you later. I'm about to hit my trap and put this shit on the clock."

"Be careful on that Mount." Red stated as he sat back on the porch. He took the blunt and lighter that Slim was handing to him.

"I already heard that bitch was on fire. But ya'll know I'm a hot boy. So, fuck it and fuck them."

Red nodded. "Hit us up to let us know that you made it to the trap safe."

"Alight, mix family."

***

Red and Slim were sitting in the living room looking at a movie called, *Never Die Alone* when Red stated that he was hungry. Hearing his stomach growl and feeling the hunger pain himself, Slim stated that he was hungry too. Not wanting to eat at the Churches Chicken located on the east side, which would be closer to Red's house, they both decided to go to McDonalds all the way on the west side near Gaston Green projects better known as Back Tha Green or BTG.

"Let me see if Baby K wants to ride with us. Go ask Tiny and her peoples If they want something from McDonalds while I go outside and get Baby K." Red told Slim.

"Tiny!" Slim yelled out as he went up the steps.

"What boy? Why you yelling my name like that?" she asked when he entered her room.

"Oh shit! Wussup Boo Thang. I ain't even know you been up here getting your hair done." Slim said. He smiled showing all 12 of his gold teeth.

"Boy wipe that Chuck E. Cheese smile off your face. What you want?" Tiny asked again.

"I want Boo Thang. Ain't that right baby girl?"

"Whatever boy. My name is Boo not Boo Thang, and you don't want me, you want ya baby mama, Lisa." Boo replied.

"See, that's where you wrong. I don't got to want Lisa, I already got her. But I want you though."

"Boy, you jokey. What you want before I call Red and tell him you up here bothering my customers." Tiny cut in.

"You sound like a hater. Anyway, me and Red about to hit Mickey D's. Ya'll boy want something?"

"Yeah, get me a quarter pounder combo and some nuggets. Oh yeah, and I want a large sprite." Tiny answered.

"How about you Boo Thang, what you want?"

"I already told you that ain't my name. You can get me a Big Mac supersize combo, 2 apple pies, and an orange drink."

"A'ight. Where ya'll money at?" he joked.

Tiny and Boo both sucked om their teeth at the same time.

"Damn ya'll, I'm just joking. We're taking Baby K with us ok?" Slim told them.

"A'ight." Tiny replied.

"Aye, Boo Thang, can I get a kiss before I go? Anything can

happen to me between here and McDonalds and you might not never see me again." Slim asked.

"Boy go on with yo' crazy self." she said laughing.

"A'ight. It's all good babe, but you gonna miss me when I'm gone." he said leaving them in the room laughing.

"I ain't know you knew Slim crazy ass." Tiny stated.

"Girl, that nigga been tryna get in my mix for the longest like for real, for real. But you know how niggas is when they on a pussy chase. I ain't got that kind of time, plus that nigga still fucking with his BM."

Tiny said, "You might as well break bread and get bread at the same time. At least you don't have to be tied down. You can do you at the same time. That nigga crushing hard. You see how that nigga been acting just now?"

"I'll keep that in mind. Now, would you come on and finish my hair, please?"

***

"Bruh, why the hell you ain't tell me Boo Thang been upstairs all that time?" Slim asked.

"Who?" Red asked.

"Boo Thang nigga!"

"Man, I don't know no damn Boo Thang. Plus, I don't be paying attention to them broads Tiny be having up there. I wish I would let Tiny catch me checking out one of her customers. I'll never hear the end of that shit."

"Man, on everything I want that bitch."

"Bruh, chill with all that. You see Baby K in the back seat."

"Right, right. But you got to get Tiny to plug me in zeek."

"You best believe Tiny already doing that." Red told him

"Mix!" Slim nodded.

"Aye check it out, I got a play in motion set up for this weekend."

"Damn my nig, you don't wasted no time init?"

"When I been up the road you and a few niggas off the Mount made sure my canteen was straight. I used to show love to a lot of nigga out here. So, since they say fuck me while I been doing my time, I'm saying fuck them too. To be honest, this is just the beginning. A lot of niggas gonna feel me and that's on everything." Red said.

"Well, I'm with ya' lil bra. You already know I ain't got no love for most of them niggas anyway. What's on your mind?" Slim asked.

"Remember G-Money from West Ashley? The one who used to come down and fuck with us from time to time before I went up the road?"

Nodding, Slim said, "Yeah. He be with Trap and them. Damn zeek, that been ya main man. So, that's who you were talking about?"

"Yeah but hold that thought. Let me order this food. What Tiny and ole girl wanted?"

Slim told Red what the ladies wanted. Then he said, "Get me the same thing Tiny got except for the nuggets and no onions. They be killing the set with them onions." Slim handed Red $20. "That's for me and Boo food."

"What you want Baby K? Your uncle Slim treating."

Kaela perked up and said, "A nugget happy meal!"

Red placed everyone's order then eased around the corner to the cashier's window. He paid, grabbed the food and made his way out of the drive thru.

"Like I was saying, I heard dawg got the Gardens on lock." Red said as they left McDonalds.

"Where he live at?" Slim asked biting into his burger.

"I'll know by tomorrow or Saturday. I'm hoping it goes down this weekend though." Red told him.

When they got back to Red's spot, Tiny and Boo were sitting downstairs in living room looking at the movie that Red and Slim had left playing. Red gave Tiny her food and Slim gave Boo hers.

"Did you miss me while I was gone?" Slim asked Boo.

"The question is did you miss me?" she answered with a question.

"Let me give you a kiss to show you how much I miss you."

"See, boy you always got to run out! Ain't nobody know where your nasty ass mouth has been." Tiny joked.

"Stay out my dawg business!" Red said.

"I swear nobody can take a joke round ya. Boo Thang, I was just joking with you. Red let's ride, I need to get back to the Mount so I can holla at Plat." Slim said.

"Come on dawg. Tiny I'll see you and Baby K later."

As they were walking out the door, Boo called out to Slim. When he turned around, she gave him a kiss on the cheek and passed him her phone number at the same time.

"How you gonna leave without giving your Boo Thang a kiss? Call me and don't make me miss you or better yet, don't miss me."

Boo teased.

"I gotcha, babe." he said with a big smile on his face.

***

Slim's son Man ran up on them as soon as Red and Slim walked through the door. Man gave them both a dap.

"Wha-thup daddy. Wha-thup uncle Red." he said mispronouncing his words due to his newly missing two front teeth.

"Wussup killa." Red said throwing a jab at him.

"Where yo momma at?" Slim asked him.

"Her in the room daddy."

"Lisa! Me and Red in here!" Slim yelled.

"A'ight!" she yelled back.

"Uncle Red, you want to play my PlayStation with me?"

"Come on lil dude. I'm about to whip yo butt."

"I'm about to hit Plat up and tell him I'm back round the way." Slim said dialing Plat number.

"Yo, wussup my nig." Plat answered.

"I'm round the way, come holla at me and don't take all day getting here."

"I'm by the corner store. I'll be there in like 10 minutes."

"Come straight to the back yard and call me when you get outside because I don't feel like hearing Lisa mouth."

Fifteen minutes later Plat was standing in the back yard with Slim.

"Make sure you carry B his shit." Slim told Plat.

"I got him. Gonna put some of this shit down first."

"You know what I want back right?"

"You said 5, right?"

"Hell no! Nigga you know what I said. Stop playing games dawg!"

Plat laughed. "I'm just joking bruh. Let me get on through before Lisa kick both our asses."

"A'ight. Hit Butta to make sure he get his shit, too."

"Damn dawg you act like you don't trust a nigga."

"I trust my momma, but I'll still check behind her to see if she do what I ask her to do, so don't take it to the heart. Especially when money is involved. Plus, that's just how I rock. No hard feelings. Feel me, family?"

"Everything's everything my nig. I'll holla at you later." Plat walked out the yard. He hit a couple of cuts and then he was gone.

Before he was out of sight, Slim was already on the phone calling Butta.

"Wussup Slim?" Butta said answering his phone.

"Plat about to bring that to you. Oh yeah, and nice looking out."

"Anytime zeek. I'll holla at you later."

CHAPTER 3

"Hello, Miss?"

"Yes, may I help you?" The nurse asked.

"Could you tell us what room Travis Green is in?"

"Are you the patient's family?"

"Yes ma'am. We're his brothers."

The nurse pressed a few keys on the computer and said, "Yes, he's in room 425 on the fourth floor. You'll need these visitor passes."

"Thank you." Both men said as they retrieved the passes and headed for the elevator.

When they entered room 425, Trap was lying in the bed in a coma. There were many tubes coming out of his body.

Tee-Tee, Trap's oldest brother said, "Damn, they fucked my lil bro up."

Slugga, the youngest brother of the three. walked up to Trap's bed with tears coming from his eyes. He touched his brother's hand and said, "I swear I'ma kill dem niggas who did this to you. You hear me! Trap, you hear me! I'ma make they pussy ass pay for this shit! I put that on everything!"

"Come on lil bra... You can't be acting like that in here. People can hear you." Tee-Tee said while grabbing Slugga by the arm.

"Man, get the fuck off of me! We got to find out who did this shit to our brother Tee-Tee! Like asap!" Slugga yelled refusing to lower his voice.

"We're going to but making loudly making threats in here ain't gonna do nothing but get us locked up quick." Tee-Tee said in a loud whisper.

"I ain't making no loud threats nigga! That's a promise!" Slugga fired back snatching away from Tee-Tee's grasp. He went over to Trap's bed and kissed his forehead. "Trap, I don't know who did this, but I swear when I do find out, it's on. They are gonna feel the same pain you felt. Just don't die on me big bro. I'll be in the car." he said as he walked pass Tee-Tee.

Tee-Tee walked to Trap's bed. "Man, lil bro, you got to pull through. Momma going crazy, Slugga going crazy, and the block going crazy. These niggas ready to ride and shoot up every hood. Momma even talking about she down to ride too. Can you picture that? Tee-Tee smiled. "It's hard seeing you like this, but I promise I'ma come here every day until you get out of here. I will be strong and hold the family and the crew together. Love ya lil bro." Tee-Tee kissed Trap's forehead.

"Man, I don't know about you but our family ain't going out like that." Slugga said.

"Going out like what nigga?" Tee-Tee exploded. "We don't even know who did it or where to start looking. All we can do is fall back and keep our ears to the street until we hear something."

Slugga exploded right back. "Man, I can't even begin to believe this shit. Un-fuckin-believable! Our fuckin brotha is laid up in the hospital with all kinds of tubes coming out of him and you're sitting here talking like everything all fuckin good!"

"Nigga, who the fuck do you think you're talking to? I been doing what you've been talking about doing, and the reason why I'm still free is because I kept a level head! I know damn well who that is laying up there in that hospital bed. You best believe I am my brother's keeper, so you damn right a nigga gonna die for this shit. But we don't know shit right now, so for now we fall back until we hear something. What good are we to Trap if we're sitting in the county jail with no bond?"

"I feel ya big bro. This shit just got me bugged out. My bad for coming off on you like that." Slugga apologized.

Tee-Tee nodded. "It's all good. I know how you feel, believe me. We just got to keep a level head. A'ight?"

"Gotcha bro."

"We got to go on the Macon and carry Meka's family some money for her funeral."

"When do you think they're gonna have the wake?" Slugga asked.

Tee-Tee said, "Probably sometime next week."

"I feel sorry for Meka's family but I'm glad it's not ours."

"Damn lil bro, that's some fuck up shit to say."

Slugga shrugged. "It's true."

CHAPTER 4

The next day Slim was posted on Read street, a dead-end street off Remount road better known as the bottom. He was chilling with Hamma, Savo, G. B, and Lil Rod when his phone started ringing. He looked at the number and saw that it was Red calling.

He answered on the third ring. "Wussup my nigga?"

"What it do big bruh? What cha got going on?" Red asked.

"Just chillin on the bottom tripping with everybody."

"Who all out there?"

"This bitch amp lil bruh! I right here with G.B., Hamma, Savo, and Lil Rod. What's good?"

"I just called to let you know I got the scoop on ole boy. That shit is going down tomorrow night. Ya dig?"

"I can dig it zeek."

"Oh, and Tiny and your Boo Thing want us to take them to the Crab Shack tonight. How you mixin'?" Red asked.

"Everything mix! You coming to get me, or I gotta drive down there?"

"Man, I don't even know why you even got a car because your ass don't ever like to drive. And you got two cars at that. That's crazy!"

Slim said, "Gas too high. So, come snatch me up. I'll be right here on the bottom."

"Aight zeek. I'll come after Tiny gets dress. Dawg, you lucky you are big bruh. Don't make this no habit." Red said.

"Yeah nigga, whatever! Get off my line."

***

Red, Tiny, Slim, and Boo were seated at a table inside of the Crab Shack eating crab legs and enjoying each other's company.

"Why you ain't call me last night?" Boo asked Slim. "You know I was waiting on your call."

"After I left ya'll yesterday I been in the house with my peoples for the rest of the night." Slim answered.

"Damn boy, you too honest for me. I like that though. I thought you would've shoot me a quick lie." Boo said.

"Lie for what? You already know I got a lil one. Plus, I ain't got shit to hide." Slim replied.

"So, Lisa know you're here with me?" Boo asked.

"You know what I mean." Slim said.

Boo playfully rolled her eyes. "Whatever nigga. You swear you got game."

"I got you." Slim said while smiling and rubbing on Boos leg under the table.

"Boy please! You ain't got me. I got you. Let's get it right."

"That's right girl! That's what I'm talking about!" Tiny said giving Boo a high five.

"That's right what?" Red interrupted. "Cause last time I checked I had your ass!" he said to Tiny.

"Well, you better check again cause my momma name Betty and the last time I checked, she had me." Tiny said snaking her neck.

"Girl, you got a smart-ass mouth you know." Red replied.

"Back to you. Where you live at Boo Thing?" Slim asked.

"I live in the Off Spree apartments by the old Roper Hospital." Boo answered.

"I know where that's at."

"I bet you do."

"When can I come through?"

"You can come through anytime. Don't nobody live with me except my daughter, but she barely be there. She be at my momma house all the time." Boo told Slim.

"Where your man at?"

"Ain't I talking to him? I told you I got you. You better know how to handle me and Lisa at the same time."

"Now look at who is spitting game." Slim said. He was impressed by her response.

Red was on the sideline ear hustling and smiling hard.

"Nigga, I don't know what you're over there smiling about! You bet not let me catch you fucking around because I'll cut ya dick off." Tiny said in a sassy manner.

Everybody busted out laughing.

***

Later that night when Red was dropping Tiny and Boo off downtown, Boo said, "Slim, I'm serious about what I said at the Crab Shack."

"I'ma call you later." Was Slim's response.

"Make sure you do that. I missed you last night."

"I swear, I got you."

"No, Slim. I got you. Now come give your Boo Thing a hug and kiss."

"Boy, Lisa gonna fuck you up." Red joked.

"Man, I got this. You're going to drop me off to my car and I'm gonna call Boo Thing and tell her I'm on my way to fuck the shit out of her tonight."

"Man, that bitch got you open already."

"She probably got me open now but watch who be open in the long run. I'ma beast between the sheets."

"Nigga, whatever. Just be ready to handle up tomorrow." Red told him.

"You already know I will. Drop me off by my house. Let me call Boo Thing right quick." Slim dialed Boo's number. "Hey babe, wussup?"

"Hey baby, wussup with you." Boo answered.

"Where you at? You still downtown?"

"Naw, I'm on my way home. You coming home tonight?"

"Home? Girl I'll call you when I get round there."

"A'ight." she replied and hung up.

"I'ma holla at you tomorrow bruh." Slim said to Red as he got out the car. He went in the house to check on Lisa and his son. Lisa was laying in their bed reading a book called, *The Coldest Winter Ever* by Sista Soulja. His son laid next to her sleeping.

"Hey baby." he said leaning down to give her a kiss.

"Hey yourself. You coming in for the night?" she asked.

"Nah. I just came to grab something right quick and check on y'all. I'm pulling a flight tonight."

"Aight. Be careful out there. My lil cousin been by here looking for you about an hour ago."

"True, I'm about to hit Read street anyway. He probably on the Bottom. Hit my jack if you need anything." he said giving her another kiss before kissing their son on the forehead.

"Please do not wake that bad ass boy up." Lisa shook her head.

Once inside of his car, Slim called his boy Jig.

"Yooo! What the mix is family?" Jig said when he answered his phone.

"This Slim, my nig. You got any of them grippas?"

"You already know. Everything going through me. I got them white G's up hoes down and some red pig faces."

"Which one is the best?" Slim asked.

Jig said, "Man, I'm snatch up on both of them mixxas and I can't move so you gotta roll on me zeek."

"Bet. Where you at?"

"Damn uh, I don't even know zeek. I'm a little fucked up right now. Hold on." Jig said.

Slim could hear Jig talking to someone in the background, then the person came on the line.

"Man, your actin!" the person said to Jig. Then he spoke into the phone. "Hello? hello?"

"Yeah, I can hear you, dawg!" Slim yelled back.

"Look ya zeek. We're at this spot behind North Charleston High school. So, mix like a twix family." Then the line disconnected.

Slim looked at his phone and said to himself, "Them niggas gotta be fucked up." He turned up his stereo and started rapping along to song called, *No Help* by Trea Tha Truth and Z-Ro.

When Slim made it to Jig's spot, there were a few women inside along with Hook, Mike D., Relly Boy, and Lil Web. They were all snatched (high of E pills) to the max. Slim came to buy two pills and it took him about thirty minutes to get them. Plus, Jig wasn't trying to let him leave until he pop one and smoke a boonk blunt (weed laced with coke) with him. When Slim got back in his car, he was already feeling the effect of the first pill, but he popped the second one anyway. He called Boo to let her know he was on the way. Boo answered her phone and told him the apartment number that she was in then hung up. Slim just looked at his phone for a minute because that was the second time that night that someone had hung up on him.

He called Boo back and said, "I'm on my way. Give me twenty minutes." Then he hung up on her.

Slim was so high that he drove thirty miles per hour the whole way to Boo's house and it ended up taking him a little over forty minutes to get there. He then called her again to let her know that he was outside.

She sucked on her teeth and said, "It took you long enough. The door been open."

When Slim walked into Boo's apartment, she yelled out that

she was in the bedroom. He followed her voice and went to the bedroom. When he walked in, Boo was laying across the bed with her legs wide open playing with herself.

"You just gonna stand there and look?" she asked as she took her finger out her pussy and sucked on it like a lollipop as she motioned for him to come to her with the other hand.

Slim's clothing seemed to magically fall off as he made his way to the bed to join Boo. She moved to the edge of the bed and pulled his dick into her mouth. He could've sworn on a stack of Bibles that she didn't have no teeth in her mouth.

"Damn baby! Let me sit down." he said after Boo been sucking him off for about five minutes.

"You like that daddy?" she asked in a sexy voice as she massaged his balls.

The mouth service that Boo was giving Slim had him sexually excited and he was ready to feel the warmness off her pussy. He told her to turn around so he could hit it from the back first.

Soon as he got his dick in as far as it could go, Boo yelled out. "Oh shit! Boy you got a big ass dick!"

Slim began grinding slow until he found his rhythm. Boo started throwing her pussy back in an attempt to match his rhythm. She shouting that she was about to cum and nutted all over Slim's dick.

"I want to lay down daddy." she panted.

They switched positions and Slim got on top. He then placed Boo's legs on his shoulders. He was high and horny and the only thing on his mind was tearing up some pussy. He started pounding Boo's back out.

"Oh lawd! Oh God this your pussy! This your pussy, Slim! I'm about to cum again! Oh God Slim I'm coming! Don't stop daddy, please don't stop!" she screamed.

Just to fuck with her head, Slim stopped in mid stroke.

"No daddy. What are you doing?" Boo whined. "Please don't stop...Come on Slim, stop playing with me for real for real."

"Whose pussy is this?" Slim asked as he started grinding slow.

"It's yours baby. Quit playing and beat this pussy up!"

Slim started pounding her pussy again. Then he stopped once more and asked her who got who.

"I got you." Boo moaned.

Laughing, Slim started stroking in and out of Boo's pussy slowly. "Who got who?" he asked again.

"Damn Slim, you got some good ass dick. Yes, right there, baby. That's my spot. Ooh this some good ass dick. What you tryna do to me?" she panted between each stroke.

"Who got who?" Was Slim's response.

"Slim, I'm coming! I swear this your pussy! This your pussy! Oh, oh, oh I'm coming!" Boo screamed as her body shook like an earthquake. Slim been hitting the pussy so hard it look like he been jumping in and out of Boo.

"Who got who?" he asked again.

Boo couldn't take it no more and yelled out. "You got me! This your pussy! You got me! Damn you got me! What is wrong with you? Why you ain't nut yet? You got to be on them pills!"

Slim just smiled and told her to get on top.

"Boy, I swear I'm gonna have to soak in the tub all night when you're finished with me."

Slim and Boo went at it for about three hours before Slim finally got his nut off. Afterwards, Boo went into the bathroom to run herself a bath. After she had soaked for a while, she came back to the bed with a wet towel and placed it between her legs.

"Boy, you beat my pussy up! You got my shit on swole you know." she smiled but she was dead ass serious.

"You fucking with a big dawg." he teased.

"You ain't never lie. But Slim listen, I already know you fuck with Lisa and that's your peoples and all that extra shit. I'm cool with that and I'm gonna play my position, but it's just gonna be about me, Lisa, and your lil man. I ain't about the drama and I swear I'll never bring drama to your doorstep so just don't bring none to mine."

"So, you really cool with that?"

"Yeah, I'm cool with it. I mean if that's what you want. It ain't like you ain't got enough dick for the both of us."

"So, I guess I got you now?"

"Ain't no guessing Slim. You got me. I'm your Boo Thing."

"Major...That's what it is then. Now, let's get some sleep before I jump back in that pussy."

"Oh, hell no you ain't! But...I can do this." she said as she slide down and pulled his dick out of his boxers and put it in her mouth.

***

Later that night, Slim had a hard time sleeping. The effects of the pills he'd taken earlier made him restless. So, he decided to get dress and leave.

"Damn, you just been gonna leave and not tell me nothing?"

Boo asked.

"Naw baby. I was gonna let you know." Slim lied. He really had no intentions of telling her anything.

"What time is it?" Boo asked.

Slim looked at the time on his phone and said, "About five something. Go on back to sleep. I'll call you later."

"Look in the top draw and get that key out there." Boo pointed towards the dresser. "That's yours. I'll talk to you later."

On the way to the mount, Slim had to pull over because he couldn't see. It felt like his eyes was crossing up on him.

"Damn, these pills got me fucked up." he said to himself.

When Slim finally made it to the bottom, he saw that niggas was still out there on the grind.

"Man, I been looking for you all day." Lisa's cousin Lil Kris said walking up to Slim. "Damn bruh, you must be snatch to the max!"

"Why you say that zeek?" Slim asked clicking his teeth together like he was cold.

"Cause you jaw jacking like a muthafucka." Lil Kris told him.

"I'm straight. What you been looking for me for?"

"I was trying to get some work, but I done holla at Plat."

"True. That's wussup. Where's Plat? He still out ya?"

"Yeah. He's at Randy's spot playing cards with D. Money, Chedda, and Scoop."

"Bet. Where Savo at with the green? I know he ain't slide yet."

"Naw. He in Randy house to."

"Aight, holla at me later when you tryna mix up again." Slim said then headed for Randy's house.

Randy's spot was the move if people wanted to chill, play cards, get out the cold or rain, or just shoot the shit with each other. Walking into Randy's house, Slim gave everybody dap and bought some green from Savo.

"My dawg mix out init?" Savo asked.

"Man, those pills Jig got are fire, zeek. Aye, Plat, I hope you ain't losing over there." Slim said referring to the card game that was going on.

"Nigga, I ain't losing a muthafuckin thing over here. You need to jump in so I can get some off your money."

"You ain't saying nothing but a word. Deal me in on the next hand."

***

Slim was so busy shooting the shit and playing cards, that he didn't realize how late, or in his case, early it was. It was after 7 a.m. when he came strolling through the door. To his surprise, Lisa and their son were already up. Lisa was in the kitchen cooking breakfast while lil man was in the living room watching TV.

"Hey baby, I'm about to take me a shower and lay it down for a couple hours." he said giving her a kiss on the cheek.

"You want some breakfast?" she asked.

"Naw baby. I'm too tired to eat." he replied and went straight to the bathroom. Thirty minutes later, he was in bed sleeping on top of the covers in his boxers.

CHAPTER 5

Tiny was in the living room looking at a movie laughing to herself when Red walked in the house followed by Baby K. They were both toting Wal-Mart shopping bags. He was frustrated because he'd been trying to call Slim since 2 p.m. with no luck, and now it was almost five o'clock.

"Tiny, call Boo and see if Slim still at her house. This nigga ain't answering his phone and he know we got shit to do tonight." Red said.

Tiny dialed Boo's number and she picked up on the first ring.

"Hey girl." Boo answered.

"Wussup, bitch. What you got going on?"

"Nothing. I'm just sitting in this house waiting on Slim ass to call me. His ass probably still sleeping."

"Well that answers that."

"Answers what?" Boo asked.

"Red asked me to call you and see if Slim was over there."

"Guuurrrlll, that nigga wore my pussy out and haul ass about 5 o'clock this morning."

"Hold on…Red! Boo said Slim left her house this morning." Tiny yelled across the house.

"Let me hold your phone right quick." Red told Tiny.

"Boo, let me call you back. And I want to hear everything wit yo nasty ass." Tiny laughed.

"Call back ho, because I got a story to tell." Boo said then hung up.

"Watch how fast Lisa answer Slim's phone if he there." Red stated.

"How you know she gonna answer that boy phone?" Tiny asked.

"Cause Slim don't got your number program in his phone." Red answered right as Lisa's line rung in his ear. She answered on the third ring with an attitude.

"Who the fuck is this and it bet not be no bitch!"

"Why the fuck is you answering my dawg phone like that girl?" Red asked.

"Boy please! Don't even play with me! You already know how I get down. Why are you calling from an unknown number anyway?" Lisa asked.

"Because I know if Slim been home you been gonna answer his phone."

"His ass got in here around seven this morning and went straight to bed. Hold on."

Red could hear Lisa calling for Slim to come to the phone.

"Yo, wussup my nigga." Slim spoke into the phone sounding like he was still half sleep.

"Dawg you need to get up and come through and hell no I ain't coming to pick you up so don't even ask."

"Aight bruh. Let me get myself together."

Red ended the call and said, "I told you that Lisa was gonna answer Slim's phone. I should've bet you on that."

"Boy you crazy. You swear you know everything." Tiny shook her head. "Oh yeah, I almost forgot to tell you that you received a letter from somebody named Cool Hand. It's on the kitchen table."

"Oh shit, that's my nigga that I did time with from Tennessee." Red said while walking towards the kitchen to get his letter. When he opened it, the only words that were written was, *I'm free nigga! Call me 901-767-5514.*

Red pulled out his cellphone and dialed the number. The phone rang a few times before Cool Hand answered.

"This got to be my nigga Red from the pen. I see you got my letter. What's up Jones?"

"What's good wit cha family? You know I had to hit you up asap. How long you been out zeek?"

"A couple of months. I had to go home and get my shit together. Remember when we had that talk when we were behind the wall?"

"So, you out doing your pimp thing?"

"Mane, you already know! I got three bitches on the stroll now. Pimpin' ain't dead, them niggas just scared, ye-ain-know?"

"I hear that pimp. Wussup with that broad who use to come see you from Tennessee?" Red asked.

"Mane, that's my bottom bitch. She had everything straight for a pimp when I touch down. So, what you got going on Jones?"

"I outcha giving these niggas hell. Remember them niggas I been telling you about? Well, the pressure is on and I giving it to them one by one. Gangsta style." Red replied.

"I hear that shit. You need to come through and check me out Jones so I can show you how it goes down in M-town." Cool Hand said.

"That sounds like a plan. Soon as I get some free time, me and my right-hand man Slim gonna come through. Lock my number in your phone and call me anytime."

"I already did. But on the cool, come through and check me playa."

"I got you. Once I handle this business, I'll plan a visit. I'll holla at you later. Be cool my nig."

"A'ight. Be easy out there, pimp."

***

Slim arrived at Red's house a little after seven that evening. On the way there, he stopped by Jig's spot to buy two E pills. The he stopped by the corner store and bought two cans of Redbull, a box of Swissers, and a pack of Newports.

"Wussup mister big stuff?" Tiny joked and smiled as she opened the door to let Slim in.

"Girl go ahead with that shit. Where Red at?"

"He's upstairs playing that game and waiting on you. You talk to my girl today? She been waiting on your call."

"Yeah. Just got off the phone with her." he said then walked past Tiny as he headed for the stairs.

Red was sitting on the edge of the bed playing Scarface on his PS3 when Slim walked into the bedroom.

"It's about time you get cha zeek." Red said as he got up to give Slim dap.

Red was wearing one of the hunting gear outfits that he had bought from Walmart. He pointed an outfit on the bed that was the same as his and told Slim to put it on.

"This how we rocking tonight." Red stated. Then he turned back to his game and began playing again.

Slim grabbed the clothes and left the room to put them on.

"I hope that shit fit." he said when Slim returned to the room.

"Yeah, they fit." Slim confirmed. "Before I got here, I stopped by Jig's spot a grab a couple of pills. You want one?"

"What kind did you get?"

"A white g's up ho's down and a red pig face."

"Yeah, I want one. Which one are you gonna throw back?" Red asked.

"We'll go half and half because both is fire. I popped one of each last night and fucked the shit out of Boo Thing. Real talk, I'm still feeling them shit right now."

"I figure that. I heard the way her and Tiny been talking on the phone. Boo got some good pussy?"

"Bruh, she got that wet-wet. For real for real, and some blazing mouth. I fucked shawty so good, I got the keys to the crib on the first night."

"That's what I'm talking about." Red said giving Slim dap.

"I got some light-light (weed) from Savo and I stopped to the store on the way here and to gct us a couple of Red Bulls and blunts. We might as well throw these pills back and smoke something before we ride out."

Red nodded and said, "Type-a-thing. Let me finish this level on this game right quick. Oh yeah, you remember that nigga I've been telling you about? The one I did time with up the road from Tennessee?"

"The pimp nigga?" Slim asked.

"Yeah."

"What about him?"

"My dawg done touch down. I just got a letter from him today and I called him up. He wants me to come over to Tennessee for a few days to kick it with him. I told him if I come, I'm bringing you with me. He was cool with that. So, I told him I'll come check him out when I get some free time."

"That's wussup, but I got to get away from Lisa first and Boo Thing cause that's my lil mix (side piece) now."

"Damn nigga! Boo got you pussy whip already." Red said shaking his head and laughing.

"I wouldn't say whipped, but that pussy good enough to keep. Plus, she down to fuck with a nigga even though I got a gal. So, it is what it is."

"I been thinking about taking Tiny with me. If that's the case, you can bring Boo too. I mean if you trying to rock like that. But you still got to work

on Lisa crazy ass. Boy Lisa gonna kill you."

"Ain't I tell you I got this? Quit worrying about Lisa nigga. I'll hit Boo Thing up and see how she feels about that. But wussup with this mix we got planned for tonight?"

"That shit about to go down. Let's throw these pills back and roll something up. I'm waiting on my lil soulja to bring me a stollo (stolen car). It's only a little after eight right now, we'll head out around 11-11:30."

"Bet. I'm about to call my Boo Thing back then."

"Nigga, I don't care what you say, your ass is pussy whipped already. Roll up before you get all lovey-dovey."

***

Red and Slim pulled up inside of the St. Andrews Garden apartment complex in West Ashley. It was a little after 12:30 a.m. when they got out the car and walked up to apartment D-12.

"You ready zeek?" Red whispered pulling his ski mask down.

"Let's do this." Slim whispered back then pulled his mask down over his face.

G-Money was just coming out of the kitchen with a plate of food and a soda when his door flew open. He screamed and threw the food at the Red and Slim and ran to the back room.

Red and Slim were right on his heels. They caught G-Money right as he was diving for the pillow on his bed. Slim lifted the pillow and grabbed the Glock 40 that G-Money was trying to get to.

"I like this." Slim said while holding up the gun.

Red made G-Money sit down on the bed. Then he slapped him across the face and G-Money started to cry.

"Stop all of that crying bitch ass nigga! Where the money and dope at?" Red demanded.

"In the corner of the closet under the carpet." G-Money whined. He was so scared that he didn't even put up a fight. "That's everything. Please don't kill me."

Slim was in the closet pulling up the carpet. G-Money wasn't lying when he said everything was in the closet. Slim found a big Glad lock bag with pills, three bricks of coke, one brick of boy (heroin), and two pounds of loud (weed) stashed the spot that G-money mentioned.

"I don't see no money." Slim yelled out from the closet.

"It's in a suitcase on the other side of the closet. Man, that's everything, please don't kill me!" G-Money begged.

"Jack pot!" Slim said when he opened the suitcase and saw the stacks of money. Red was pissed because G-Money didn't put up a fight. He wanted a reason to shoot G-Money and since he didn't have one, he took his mask off.

"Why Red? Why are you doing this to me man?" G-Money asked with confusion and fear in his eyes.

"Because you a bitch ass nigga and don't know the meaning of loyalty. That's why."

"C-come on Red. I th-th-thought we been be-be-better than that." G-Money stuttered.

"How could you even think that after ya'll boy left me hanging when I went to jail? Ol' bitch ass nigga." he said then slapped the fire out of G-Money again.

Slim emerged from the closet carrying two suitcases. "I got every-" he paused when he saw that Red wasn't wearing his mask.

"You see that nigga right there?" Red pointed at Slim. "That's my dawg. My muthafuckin round. He held me down when ya'll clowns forgot about me." he slap G-Money again. "Slim, go head and take your mask off so this pussy can take a look at a real nigga. Go ahead Slim, take the mask off. He ain't gonna tell nobody. I know you remember Slim, don't you?"

G-Money didn't answer fast enough and that made Red slap him again. This time drawing blood from his left eye. G-Money shook his head up and down vigorously in a silent response to Red's question.

"Man, I swear you's a pussy. Good word!" Red said and started raining punches all over G-Money's face.

Slim was looking at Red like he was crazy. He felt like Red was doing too much. Especially since they had already gotten what they came for.

"Man, dead that nigga and let's slab out this mix. We got what we came for." Slim said making his way to the front door.

Red put his gun to G-Money head and said, "You might as well pray to me because I'm your God now. Oh, and here's something to take to the grave with you. That shit that happened to Trap and Meka...we did that." he then shot G-Money in the head two times and kicked him to make sure he was dead. Red ran out of the apartment to catch up with Slim, who was waiting outside with the car running.

On the drive back to Red's spot. Slim noticed Red rocking back and forth like he was wrapped up in a strait jacket.

"Man, what the fuck is wrong with you?" Slim asked.

"Dawg, it's them pills. I swear I'm high as a muthafucka and I can't keep still for shit." Red answered.

"Man, you crazy ya know. If you could've seen the way you spazzed out back there, you would've thought you were somebody else."

"Real talk, something just came over me, zeek. Those pills been talking to me and telling me to show that nigga my face. I already knew I would've had to kill him when I took my mask off, so I was like fuck it. It is what it is. What made me so fucking mad is that the nigga ain't even put up a fight. That nigga started crying like a bitch. What type of nigga is that? Where they do that at?"

Before Slim could answer, Red said, "I'll tell you what kind of nigga he is. He's a dick in the booty ass nigga that don't deserve to breathe the same air that I breathe. Hell, the same air we breathe. That's why I wanted him to see our faces, because I wanted him to see what a real nigga looked like and I wanted him to see his executioner so he'll know how to be a real nigga in the afterlife or he gonna meet a nigga like me again. Like Tupac said, *A coward dies a thousand times*."

"What? Nigga, you gone off those pills. Did you just hear the shit that just came out of your mouth? That's your last time poppin before we go on a lick." Slim said laughing.

"What-the-fuck-ever nigga, I feel good."

***

Slim and Red were in at the kitchen table counting the money from the lick they just came up off.

"Two hundred and fifty stacks." Red announced after counting the last stack in his hand.

"What we gonna do with this boy (heroin)? Because I don't know nothing about selling this shit." Slim asked.

"I don't know how to sell that shit neither. Fuck it, we'll just worry about that later. As a matter of fact, ain't Jig cousin Bone be selling that shit?"

Slim shrugged and said, "Hell if I know. Dawg be having his hands in all kind of shit. But I'll hit him up because I been meaning to hit him up anyways. I'll do that tomorrow."

Red nodded his head towards the bag on the table. "Yeah, do that. How many pills in that bag?"

"You must want me to guess that number because I damn sure ain't about to it here and count all those pills tonight. What I am going to do is pop one, though. These are those Dope Boy Magic ones too!"

"Dope Boy Magic?" Red asked.

"The pills with the sparkles in them."

"Oh, I heard about them but I ain't never knew what they were called."

"I'm about to call Boo Thing and get in her mix. You good right?" Slim asked after they finish splitting everything.

"Yeah nigga. You already know. Just be careful riding like that."

Slim thought about what Red said. "You know what, I'ma just call Boo Thing and tell her to come pick me up."

"Yell upstairs when you leave so I can lock my door. I about to go tear Tiny ass off. I'm horny as hell. Make sure you hit Bone up tomorrow."

"Bet."

After Red disappeared up the stairs, Slim pulled out his cell and dialed Boo Thing's line.

"Hello." Boo answered in a sexy voice.

"Hey babe. I need you to come get me."

"You alright? Come get you from where?" she asked.

"Everything good, babe. I'm downtown at Red house and I don't feel like driving."

"Okay. I'm getting up now."

"Bet. I'll see you when you get here."

Fifteen minutes later, Boo Thing was parked outside waiting on Slim.

"Red! Come lock the door! My ride outside!" Slim yelled from the foot of the steps.

"Go head bruh! I got it!" Red yelled back.

When Slim got into Boo's car, he put one of the suitcases from the robbery in the back seat.

"What happened? Lisa done put you out?" Boo asked.

"Nah. I just got a couple of my things in there. Could you take me to Dave's restaurant? I'm hungry. You want something outta there? I'm about to call in my order."

"Yeah. Get me a fish sandwich meal with fried shrimp and one of those fruit punch Mystic drinks."

After Boo and Slim picked up their food, they headed back to Boo's house. They sat on her bed eating and talking.

"What you do all day, babe?" Slim asked.

"I went by my momma house to check on her and my daughter. When I got back home, I cleaned my house and watched TV." Boo replied.

"That's wussup. I ain't even gonna lie. When I left here this morning I been so mix up. I don't even know how I'm eating now because I'm still snatched. All I want to do is eat this food and lay up with you."

"You want to watch a movie until we fall asleep?"

"That sounds like a plan. Oh yeah, I meant to ask you earlier when I was talking to you on the phone, but me and Red thinking about going to Tennessee soon and he taking Tiny so if you ain't busy you can come with me."

Boo smiled and said, "I'm cool with that. I got some vacation time at my job. Just let me know when."

"Bet."

"Which movie you want to watch?"

"Let's watch something funny. I done seen enough gangsta shit for the night."

"Ok, well we can watch *Dance Flick*. I like that movie."

"I'm cool with that."

"If you wake up in the morning and I'm not here I'll be at church." Boo told him as she placed the movie into the DVD player. She joined him on the bed and cuddled up next to him as the movie began to play.

CHAPTER 6

"What's good?" Red asked when he answered his phone.

"Rise and grind family. I just got off the phone with Bone." Slim replied.

"Oh yeah? What that nigga talking about?"

"Zeek say we could get about 80 stacks off that ming (heroin) if we sell the whole thing at one time."

"Shid, that's the business. See if he want to buy it and we'll just throw him a deal. While you do that, I'll count the pills."

"Ok, I'll hit you back." Slim told him.

Moments later, Red's phone rung.

"What he say?" Red asked when Slim called him back.

"First he asked how much we wanted for that ming. I told him seventy thousand, but he offered sixty. So, I told him it was a deal since it's basically free money. He's gonna meet me, so I need to come get my car and snatch that up from you. Just make sure everything is ready." Slim told him.

***

Slim had Boo drop him off at Red's house.

"Hold on babe." Slim said as he got out of the car. "I want you to ride behind me." he said before closing the car door. Then he ran to Red's front door and knock two times. Red open the door to let Slim in. On the front room table, he saw that Red had been separating the pills and bagging them up.

"How many pills we come off with?" Slim asked.

"4,974. Some of them ming been crush up. Plus, we threw one back last night. We probably been at five thousand before that. I'm bagging em up in packs of one hundred. We got a little something-something left over that we can hit later." Red told him.

"That's wussup. Where Tiny at?" Slim asked.

"She went to pick up one of her customers."

"True. Let me get on through. I got Boo Thing outside waiting to follow me back up the road, so let me get that ming."

"What you got going on later?" Red asked handing Slim a Footlocker bag with a Nike shoe box in it.

"Before I go home I'ma shoot back up ya to bring you your check. Then I'ma go spend some time with Lisa and my son. Boo just got out of church and she supposed to be going to her ol' lady house to chill with her daughter."

"You can go head home. I'll stop by there later and bring your half of them pills and I'll get my check then." Red said.

"Bet it up. I'll holla at you later then." Slim said. Just as he was walking out of the door, his cellphone rang. He looked at the number on his phone, it was his dude Bone. "Wussup B?"

"I outcha. What building you in zeek?" Bone asked.

"Park in front of the D building. I'm coming right now. I had to make a quick run."

"Look ya zeek! Where you at? I got too much bread on me to be outcha fucking around." Bone asked.

"I'm riding towards you now my nigga. Give me like ten to fifteen minutes."

"You got me outcha dawg. For real for real. I'ma go over to this lil broad spot I know that stay around here. She lives in E-7. Just come there." Bone told him.

"A'ight. Bet." Slim ended the call.

When Slim and Boo turned into the Off-Spree apartment complex, he pulled to the side and told Boo to go ahead to her spot. Then he grabbed the Footlocker bag from his car and made his way to apartment E-7.

"You better get you another watch if you think that was fifteen minutes." Bone stated after opening the door.

"Man, stop complaining so damn much. Who in ya with you?" Slim asked looking around.

"Just me and ol' girl. Let me see what you working with." he said opening the bag Slim handed to him. "Grab that bookbag off the chair. Everything's there. You can count if you want to."

"If the check ain't right I'll be calling you. I got some white too if you want any." Slim told him.

"I'm straight right know on that, but I'll look you up when I need a bitch or two. If this lil nigga ain't right, I'll be on yo jack asap."

"I ain't even sweating that because everything is good. But hit me up when you ready to get up with these bitches (cocaine). They bad too." Slim said giving Bone dap on the way out the door.

When Slim walked into Boo's apartment she was coming out

the bedroom. She no longer had on the church clothes she'd worn earlier. She was now sporting a pair of Baby Phat jeans and a shirt to match. Her feet were adorned with a pair of Baby Phat wedge sandals showing off her pretty petite pedicured feet.

"Baby, I'm about to go. Can I have a couple of dollars?" she asked sliding on her Donna Karon shades. Slim reached in his pocket and gave her one hundred and fifty. "Thank you." she kissed him.

After Boo left, Slim grabbed the suitcase he'd brought with him. He pulled out his clothes and laid them across the bed, then he went to take a shower. After he was done, he got dress, grabbed the suitcase, his bookbag, and headed home to be with Lisa and Man.

***

Red was in his living room looking at *First Sunday* smoking a blunt and laughing at Katt Williams when Tiny came through the front door with one of her customers.

"Damn, Red! Why you always got to be smoking that stink ass shit?" Tiny argued.

"Tiny, don't start with me. When your momma bringing Baby K home?"

"Tonight, or tomorrow. This is Kiesha, Kiesha this is Red. Go head upstairs to the room on the left. I'm right behind you." After her client was out of earshot, Tiny turned to Red and said, "Are you going anywhere any time soon?"

"Naw. I'm playing the house for the day. Why wussup?"

"Just asking. Let me get her out the way."

Red phone started ringing. When he looked at the caller I.D., he saw that it was his homie Dolla calling. "Wussup Dolla Bill?"

"What da mix is Red? I need to see you like asap. I hope you ain't north mixin' (in the north area)."

"Naw zeek. I'm on Johnson St. projects."

"Major! I about to roll on you family. Same order."

"Bet."

Red was upstairs bagging up the last ounce when Dolla called and said he was outside. He went down to let him in and Dolla came in carrying a McDonald's bag in his hand.

"Damn you stay with a bag from Micky D's. You act like you work there and you deliver for them." Red joked.

"Cut it out, bruh. I make too much money to be working at Micky D's. My lil people's work there. I gotta ass of these bags. When I make moves this how I be rockin".

"I'm just trippin, bruh. It don't make me no difference to me. Here you go." Red said handing him the product.

"Dawg, I got to bring you a triple beam. I know that little clock be killing you." Dolla said referring the scale that Red had been using to weigh the drugs.

"Nah, it don't be killing me but if you can get me a triple beam, I'll buy it."

"I got one you can hold on to. I'll bring it through later."

Nodding, Red said, "Nice looking out. Oh yeah, I got them grippas. I'll let you get em for the low-low."

"What kind you got?"

"Slim say they call em' Dope Boy Magic."

"I heard them shit the truth. How much you talking?" Dolla asked.

"$2 a piece, but I'll let you get them for $1 a piece but you gotta buy one hundred at a time."

"True that. When I bring the beam back I'll snatch a couple packs. I'll call when I'm on my way back." he replied giving Red dap.

"For anybody else, I want three a pop." Red stressed before letting Dolla hand go.

"Bet. I'll get at you later fam."

A few hours later, Tiny came down the stairs.

"Red, you want to ride with me to drop her off?" Tiny asked.

"Yeah, because I need you to take me on the Mount anyways."

"I ain't say nothing about doing all that." she joked.

"Whatever girl. Let's ride."

Tiny and Red left out of the house together and got into Tiny's car. After dropping her client off, Tiny asked Red where he needed to go on the Mount.

"Take me by Slim house right quick, then I need to holla at two of my lil niggas." Red then pulled out his cell and made a call.

"Wussup Lil V?" Red said when the picked up.

"Who dis?" Lil V asked.

"Red, zeek! How you rockin'?"

"Everything mix. Me and D-Money been gonna call you when he got back from catching his sale. We're ready to see you."

"I'm on my way to the Mount now. I'll call you when I reach Slim's spot."

"A'ight big family. Aye, you gonna do the same thing again?" Lil V asked referring to getting another front.

"We'll talk in a second." Red replied before hanging up. Then he called Slim.

"Wussup, lil bruh?" Slim answered.

"How you rockin', zeek?"

"I'm right here playing this game with my son."

"Me and Tiny about to be pulling up in your yard."

"Lisa, open the door!" Slim yelled. "Ya'll just come in. The door will be open."

Minutes later, Tiny and Red arrived at Slim's place.

"Come on." Red said to Tiny as he exited the car.

"Go ahead and do you. I'll be waiting in the car." Tiny replied.

"Girl, you be acting funny." Red shook his head and closed the door.

"Where Tiny at? I thought ya'll came together." Slim asked when Red walked into the house.

"Her jokey (funny acting, dumb or sickening) ass stayed in the car. Let me spit at you, though."

"Damn Red, you can't speak when you walk in my house?" Lisa argued as she emerged from the kitchen.

"My bad L. Wussup, wit' cha sis? Where my nephew at?"

"He's in that room. I thought Slim said Tiny was with you. I wanted to know if she could do my hair this week."

"Go ask her. She right outside in the car."

Once Lisa had left the room, Slim said, "Wussup?"

"I need to borrow nine zones right quick. Then I need Lil V. and D-Money to meet me over here. Here's the pills. I got em all bag up in one hundred count packs."

"I got the zones for you, but Lisa and Man are here. You gotta meet them boy somewhere else. I ain't rocking like that. Let me get this bread for you." Slim told him.

"While you're back there, break it down into two separate 4 ½'s." Red said before Slim left the room.

Red was in Man's room playing the PlayStation with him

when he heard Slim yell out. "Out there ain't hot! Today is Sunday!"

Sucking his teeth. Red yelled back, "Whatever nigga. Everyday hot round this bitch!"

"Man, go head in the back yard and handle yo business. If Lisa catch you, you're on your own and I'ma act like I don't know nothing." Slim said walking into Man's room

"Nice looking big bruh." Red said hopping on his phone to call Lil V. "Yo, is D. Money back?"

"Yeah he right here."

"Bet. You know that trailer park behind Slim's house?"

"Yeah."

"Call me when you get to the gate."

***

After Red got through talking with Lil V. and D-Money, he went back into the house to give Slim dap so he could leave. When he walked outside, Lisa and Tiny were still sitting in the car. Lisa got out the car smiling with a cloud of smoke trailing behind her as Red approached them.

"Girl, I ain't know you smoke weed." he said.

"There's a lot of shit you don't know about me. I put a lil something in the air every once in a while. Tiny, I'll be down your way between Tuesday or Wednesday to get my hair done." Lisa told her.

"Just call me." Tiny said putting the car in drive.

"No wonder why your jive ass ain't wanted to come in. Your ass had want to get high. That bet not be none of my green neither with ya'll slick ass. As soon as I told Lisa you were outside she haul ass out the door."

"Nigga, you ain't slick neither! We saw you at the back gate. The only reason she ain't said nothing was because we been too busy tripping off your ass."

"Whatever." he said sucking his teeth, knowing he was busted. Just then, his phone started ringing. He looked at his caller I.D. and saw that it was Dolla.

"Wussup Dolla Bill?"

"I'm on your side of town. I about to come through."

"I'm on the interstate coming from the Mount. Give me about fifteen minutes."

"Bet. I want two packs instead of one. I'll be on the P (projects) waiting on you." Dolla Bill told him.

"Roger that." Red said before ending the call.

When Red finally made it back to his place, he and Dolla Bill handled business. They chopped it up for a bit, then walked him to the door and he left. Tiny was on the couch watching TV and Red decided to join her.

"Is Baby K coming home tonight?" he asked.

"Nope! We got the house to ourselves tonight." she answered with a smile.

Red looked her up and down, then said, "I don't know what you smiling for. We ain't fucking tonight."

Tiny rolled her neck as she replied with, "Oh yes the hell we are, and I want a half a pill."

"So, you poppin now?"

"Damn! I can't pop a pill with my man?"

"I ain't tripping, but you bet not let me find out."

"Find out what?! Boy, go ahead and get the pill and quit actin! You know you want to roll with me." Tiny told him.

"Since you want to roll with a big dawg you poppin the whole thing. We ain't faking. Go pour us some orange juice, too. Don't start acting stupid when you start grippin (feeling the high)."

Tiny went to fetch the orange juice. When she came back, Red gave her one of the pills..

"Why is it sparkling like that?" she asked.

"You gonna pop it or what? Come on, let's throw em back at the same time. You ready?"

Tiny shook her head up and down as she put the pill on her tongue. Red did the same thing and they both took a sip from their glass of juice and swallowed their pills at the same time.

"Come on. Let's go upstairs and look at TV until this pill kick in." Red suggested.

"No, let's stay right here."

"Alight. Let me cut the lights off then. You straight? You want to smoke a blunt?" Red asked.

Tiny frowned a little. "I'll pop a pill with you, but I ain't smoking no stink ass boonk."

"Girl, I ain't talking about no fucking boonk! You crazy! We gonna smoke some reg (weed) and chill until our pill kick in."

"Oh, aight that's cool."

By the time they'd finish smoking, the effects of the pills started to kick in. Tiny was the first to feel her high and she began rubbing on herself while making sexy moaning sounds that caught Red's attention.

"Gurl, don't start acting stupid up in ya." he said while looking at her funny.

"Come here boy." she said grabbing him roughly.

"Hold on, baby let me put on some music right quick." he said picking up the remote. Red pushed the mute button for the tv, then he picked up the stereo remote and turned it on. He went over to the stereo and shuffled through the CD's until he came across one by Michael Watts called *Fuck Action 40*. Placing the CD into the player, he pushed play and Fantasia's voice came through the speakers singing her song, *Truth Is*.

The whole time he been messing with the stereo, Tiny was all up on him with her hand up under his shirt rubbing on his chest and pinching his nipples. Once he had the music playing, she pushed him back onto the couch and began sucking on his nipples. She was on fire. She started unbuckling his pants and kissing her way down chest towards his belly button.

Red was getting horny as hell by the minute. He pulled his shirt up over his head and threw it on the floor. It felt like every place Tiny put her mouth set off electricity through that part of his body.

Tiny was trying to pull Red's pants off when he stopped her and told her to take her clothes off first. She stood up and danced slowly to the music as she took her time removing her clothes. Red watched with anticipation while jacking his dick. When she stepped out of her thong, she positioned herself between his legs and got down on her knees. Tiny took Red's dick into her mouth and began sucking him. At first it was slow and sensual, but once she found her rhythm, she became a beast.

"Oh shit, baby." he moaned.

"You like that baby?" she asked teasing the tip of his dick with her tongue.

Red's body went into convulsion. Tiny was in a zone. She started licked up and down the shaft of his dick like it was a freeze pop.

"Please bring that pussy here." he begged.

Tiny got up to straddle Red's dick, but he stopped her.

"No baby, I want to taste you first. Suck my dick while I eat your pussy." he told her.

Red began eating Tiny's pussy like it was his last meal while she went to work on his dick. Red licked his finger, making them nice and wet with his saliva. Then slowly slid it in her ass and started fingering her asshole while he sucked on her clit at the same time.

"I'm coming baby! Don't stop! I'm coming!" Tiny screamed in ecstasy.

"Let me taste it baby."

"Here it comes baby! Oh my gawd, here it comes!" she screamed. Her legs shook uncontrollably as she came all over Red's face and mouth.

"Get up and bend over the arm of the couch." Red demanded as he stood up to position himself behind Tiny. Just when he slid into her wet pussy, R. Kelly's *12 Play* began to play.

"Spank me daddy!" she moaned. Red obliged and smacked her hard on her ass cheek. "Oh baby! Do it again." she begged.

Red smacked her ass again.

"Harder baby, smack me harder!"

He did as he was told and smacked Tiny's ass over and over. He smacked her so hard that he could see the red handprints on her skin.

"Fuck me daddy! Get this pussy!" she said throwing her pussy back at him. "Red, I'm coming! I'm coming!"

Tiny's pussy was so wet that Red's dick kept sliding out of

her.

"Sit down." she instructed. "Let me get on top."

Red sat on the couch and Tiny climbed on top of him cowgirl style. He had to slouch down a little bit to get right. After positioning herself on top of him, Tiny slid down his dick and started working him like she was riding a bull. He had to grip her ass to get her to calm down. He had one of her titties in his mouth at the same time sucking on her nipple like a newborn baby.

"Oh shit," he moaned with her breast still in his mouth. "I'm about to come."

In one swift motion, Tiny jumped off of his dick and began sucking him. Her sex game was so intense. Red was moaning like a bitch as he shot his load into her mouth. Without missing a beat, she kept on sucking swallowing his cum at the same time. The sensitivity was too much for Red so he snatched his dick out of her mouth.

"Damn girl! You think you a vampire or something?!"

"No, but I'll be your vampire tonight. I want some more dick."

"Let me get some rest. We got all night."

"I know we got all night. I'm trying see if you can make it to the morning."

Red was tired as hell, but he was never one to turn down a

challenge. He told Tiny that he was going to grab himself some water real quick. When he returned, Tiny was waiting for him with her ass in the air.

"Come get this pussy, daddy." she smiled back at him.

Red grabbed his dick and licked his lips. He joined her on the couch and took his position.

CHAPTER 7

Trap woke up on a Monday morning not knowing where he was at. He couldn't talk due to the tube that was in his throat. Looking around the room, he figured that he was in a hospital. At that moment, a nurse came walking into his room doing her rounds and noticed that he was awake. She left out of the room in a hurry to get his doctor.

"Nice to have you back with us Mr. Green. I'm doctor Jones and this is Nurse Byus. If you give me a second, we're gonna run a few tests and then remove the tube from your mouth so you'll be able to talk."

Dr. Jones and Nurse Byus began checking and recording Trap's vitals. Once they were done, they began removing the tube from his throat. Dr. Jones had him do a short breathing exercise to get his throat muscles to relax before he started speaking.

After taking a few sips of water that the nurse had given him, Trap asked, "How long have I been here?"

"You were brought in here Thursday morning. Do you know what today is Mr. Green?"

Trap shook his head no.

"Today is Monday, Mr. Green. You're a fighter. We almost lost you. We thought you weren't gonna make it. Your two brothers have been coming here every day since you were brought in. Two detectives have also been by daily. I'm supposed to notify them once you regained consciousness, but you look like you could use a little more rest. I'll just notify your family first."

* * *

When Trap woke up, two detectives were in his room.

"How are you doing Mr. Green? I'm Detective Deckerd and this is my partner Detective Cummbee. We would like to ask you a few questions if you don't mind."

Trap didn't say anything. He just looked at the detectives with a blank expression on his face.

"Do you know the person or persons who did this to you?" Detective Deckerd asked.

Trap remained silent.

"Do you know why?" Detective Deckerd asked trying again.

Silence.

"Are you in some kind of street beef with anyone?" Detective Deckerd asked now becoming frustrated.

More silence.

"Why would someone kick in your door, damn near torture you to death, shoot you three times, and kill Ta'Meka Washington?!" Detective Cummbee asked jumping in because he was tired of his partner asking questions and not getting any answers.

Up until that moment, Trap didn't know Meka was dead. He closed his eyes as tears rolled down his face.

"Yeah! I know what the deal is! You ain't nothing but a drug dealer and because of you, an innocent young lady was killed! Yeah, that's right Trap! I know all about your whole family!" Detective Cummbee taunted him.

"Calm down detective! Get a hold of yourself. You are way out of line." Detective Deckerd interjected.

At that moment, Doctor Jones, Tee-Tee, and Slugga walked into Trap's room.

"What's going on here detectives? My patient is not well. He just came out of his coma. You all said that you just wanted to ask him a few questions not upset him."

"That's what we are doing doctor." Detective Deckerd stated.

"Well, it doesn't look like that's what your partner is doing. I cannot have you stressing out my patient. As I said before, he's not well. I'm going to have to ask you to come back another day when he is in better condition."

"We do apologize doctor. We'll be back to see you soon, Mr. Green." Detective Deckerd said as he ushered his partner towards the door.

"How you doing Tee-Tee? Long time no see. Where have you been hiding?" Detective Cummbee asked sarcastically.

"I ain't hiding. I just been working and taking care of the family." Tee-Tee answered with a smile on his face matching the detective's sarcasm.

"Yeah, whatever." Detective Cummbee said, then walked out the hospital room with Detective Deckerd right behind him.

"I've been trying to get that guy for the longest but he keeps slipping through the cracks." Detective Cummbee said as he and

Detective Deckerd walked through the hospital hallway.

"Who?" Detective Deckerd asked.

"Tyrone Green, also known as, Trigga T or Tee-Tee."

"What's the story on him?"

"Shit! Where should I start? He did a juvenile life stint for a murder back in 94', got out in 97'. Caught another murder charge in 02'. Lucky son-of-a-bitch beat the charge in the preliminary hearing. Not enough evidence to convict. Never made it to court. Then just when I thought I had him for ABWIK (assault and battery with the intent to kill) in 03' the fucking witness change their statement."

"So, I guess you got a real hard on for this guy?"

"Hell yeah! You better believe it! This guy is a piece of work. I put my badge on it that some shit is about to hit the fan. They probably got something to do with that murder that happen over the weekend in West Ashley."

"Well, that's not our jurisdiction. Also, keep in mind that Travis Green is the victim and his brothers are his family. So, quit making it look like they are the suspects."

"Say what you want, but I'm gonna keep my eye on that Green clan."

***

"Wussup, lil bruh? Glad to see you back with us. Damn you had us scared for a minute." Tee-Tee said.

"Yeah man, you had us worried like a muthafucka!" Slugga stressed. "You already know I been ready to shoot up the whole Chuck, but Tee-Tee had to talk some sense into me."

"That's my cue to leave." Dr. Jones interjected. "I'll give you all some time to talk. Remember guys, only one hour because Mr. Green needs to get plenty of rest." Then Doctor Jones left the room.

"Man Trap, what's really going on? Do you know who did this shit?" Tee-Tee asked soon as the door shut.

"I don't know shit, bruh. All I know is me and Meka were in the back room and somebody knocked on the door. I got up to look through the peephole, and the next thing I know I'm on the floor with two muthafuckas standing over me with bandannas over their faces. Man, they killed Meka!" Trap said as tears fell from his eyes.

"Me and Tee-Tee carried some money over there to help out with the funeral. Look here bruh, hurry up and get up outta here so we can give hell to the niggas who did this to you. The police told momma you got tortured. What they do to you?" Slugga asked.

"They stabbed me in both my legs. My right leg is fucked up the most because dude stabbed me twice in it. The doctor say I'ma walk with a slight limp because that fucka cut a nerve. Man, those muthafuckas burn my dick with one of them torch lighter. I swear that's the worst pain I've ever felt. I told them where the stuff and money was at and they still tried to kill my ass. After that, everything else is a blur. I woke up in here today with three bullet holes in me." Trap shook his head, then whispered, "Damn they killed Meka."

"Her funeral is Thursday and they're having the wake tomorrow and Wednesday. Don't worry about that other shit, we can always get that back. We just need you to pull through right now. Momma worried about you, too." Tee-Tee said.

"What's up with momma anyways? Why she ain't come with ya'll?" Trap asked.

"You know momma. She said she ain't tryna see you laid up in no hospital." Slugga answered.

"Excuse me fellas. Times up. Mr. Green needs to take his meds." Doctor Jones said walking into the room.

Slugga and Tee-Tee bumped fists with Trap and told him they'll be back tomorrow. As they were walking out of the room, Trap told them to send his condolences to Meka's family and to let her mom know that he loved Meka.

"We got you, bruh." Tee-Tee assured him.

***

"Why you ain't tell Trap about G-Money?" Slugga asked once they were back in the car.

"Because, you already see how bruh been trippin ova Meka." Tee-Tee answered.

"Yeah, you right. Man, they catch G-Money down bad init?"

"Fuckas caught my dawg in his stash house. On the real, I think the same people who did that shit to Trap killed G-Money too."

"Who the fuck is these niggas?" Slugga asked out loud but meaning to say it to himself.

"Between Trap and G-Money, they got too much shit for nobody not to know what's going on. I know somebody know something." Tee-Tee stated.

Slugga shook his head and said, "We gotta make them tell us, bruh. We done try your way for four days now. If we don't hear something by the time that Meka's funeral is over with, then we gonna try my way."

Tee-Tee turned to Slugga for a second then turn back to look at the road. It took him a few minutes to speak. When he did, he only said three words. "Bet it up."

CHAPTER 8

"Wussup Zeek?" Red said answering his phone knowing that it was Slim on the other end.

"What's good with you my nig? What you got going on for today?" Slim asked.

"Just right ya chillin'. Tiny went to the grocery store. So, I'm up in here playing this game."

"Me and Mann about to go to Northwoods Mall. You and Baby K wanna to meet us out there?"

"Bet. That sounds like a plan. Ya'll about to leave now?"

"No. I got to wait until he gets out of school. I'll hit you back round 3:30pm."

"A'ight. Just hit me when you're ready."

"Bet. I'll holla at you later. Somebody on my other line." Slim said then he clicked over. "Who this?"

"Platinum Stacks my nig." Plat replied.

"What's good Plat?"

"You. I need to see you."

"I'm in the hood on B-Dub (Blackwell St.). Come on through."

"Me and Lil Kris together."

"A'ight."

"What happen to you yesterday? I been blowing up your phone." Plat said when he entered Slim's house.

"I been doing so much rippin and runnin I had to give my body some rest for a few days. But what's on your mind?"

"You know what time it is. Oh yeah, before I forget, Peter Man say call him. He been looking for you too."

"Wussup Lil Kris?"

"Man, I'm just tryna get in where I fit in." Lil Kris answered.

"Look here Kris, I'ma fuck with you but just because you're

Lisa's cousin don't mean I won't beat your ass up. Give me a second."

When Slim came back into the room, he gave Plat the nine zones he requested, and Plat handed him the money he owed him. Then he gave Lil Kris two and a baby (two ounces and a quarter spoon) and a hundred pack of pills.

"Check it Kris, I want $2100 back for the two and a baby, and $200 back for the pills. Kris, don't play with my money, bruh."

"I got you man. Why you on me like that zeek?" he asked.

"Because one, your ass stay in and out of jail and I want my money even if you get locked up. Two, you my gal cousin and I don't want you to think you can come at me short."

"Whatever, bruh. I ain't about to play fuck up. Can you cook this up for me though?" Kris asked.

"I got you." Plat spoke up. "Let's ride."

"Ya'll be easy out there." Slim stated closing the door behind them. Then he dialed Peter Man's number.

"Who this?" Peter Man asked when he answered his phone.

"This Slim, zeek. Wussup?"

"Man, where you at dawg? I need to see you asap. I been calling you since Sunday night. Rell said he just hollered at you earlier that day."

"Yeah. Him and Butta caught me before I turned my phone off. My bad bruh, I should've checked on you. I'm out here on B. Dub now. Come through right quick."

"I'm coming right now. Have me ready so I can stop and go."

"Bet." Slim said then hung up.

While Slim waited on Peter Man to come through, he called Lisa.

"Hey baby, wussup? Where you at? You been gone all day." he said when she answered her phone.

"I told you yesterday that I had something to do today. I'm on the Macon. A friend of mine got killed Thursday morning in that home invasion and I'm over here with the family. Her wake is tonight. That's why I told you to watch Mann all day."

"Who's your friend that got killed?"

"Her name is Meka."

"Oh, yeah. I heard about that shit. Ain't her and that nigga Trap get shot up?"

"Yeah. They got Trap in MUSC. He just came out his coma. They say he got fucked up bad. Let me go. We'll talk later."

"A'ight, I was just calling to check on you."

"Okay baby. Love you."

"Love you too." he responded. Then he hung up and called Peter Man back.

"Where you at zeek?" he asked when Peter Man answered.

"I'm in front of your gate. You coming out or I got to come in?"

"I'm coming out. I got to walk and meet my son after school anyways."

Once they got through handling their business Peter Man asked Slim if he wanted a ride to pick up his son.

"You can drop me off. We'll walk back."

After Slim picked Mann up from school, they stop by the ice cream parlor across the street from the school. As they were coming out they ran into Chedda, Slam Black, and Slow Mo.

"Wussup ya'll." Slim dapped them up.

"Wussup ya'll.." Mann said mimicking his father.

"What's good Slim?" Everybody said in unison as they all gave Mann dap.

"Chedda, let me holla at you for a second." Slim said.

"Ya'll go head in. I'll be right behind you. Order me a chilli dog with mustard and french fries." she said to Slam Black and Slow Mo. "Wussup, bruh?"

"How you mixxin out ya?" Slim asked.

"I ain't making no major moves, but I'm doing me big family." Chedda replied.

"I was gonna holla at you the other day when I saw you outside of the corner store. Anyway, I'ma call you later today, I got a lil something for you."

"That's wussup. Just hit me up when you ready zeek. You know Tasha about to come home right?"

"When?"

"Between the beginning of next month or the month after that. You know how people are about telling their release date. She tryna pop up on everybody."

Slim nodded and said, "Type-a-thing. I'ma get on through, I'm taking this knuckle head to the mall. Chedda, whatever I do for you is between me and you zeek."

"I don't be putting people in my business boy!"

"A'ight. That's all I wanted to hear. I'll holla." Slim said walking off.

"Daddy, you like Chedda?" Mann asked.

"What!? No. I don't like Chedda. Well, at least not like that. Why you ask me that?"

"Cause she a girl."

Slim laughed and said, "I don't have to like her just because she's a girl."

"Well, I like her and she gonna be my girlfriend." Mann said with a smile on his face.

"Boy! You wouldn't even know what to do with Chedda. Wit yo lil ass. Besides, I think Chedda would rather be your homeboy then your girlfriend. Come on, lets hurry up and get to the house." Slim said laughing.

Walking down B. Dub, Slim cell phone started ringing. He looked at the caller I.D. and saw that it was Jig.

"Wussup zeek?" he asked when he answered.

"Damn mix! It's like that?" Jig replied.

"Nigga, what the fuck are you talking about? It's like what?"

"I been on the Mount today and I ran into Lil Kris ass…"

"…and he told you I got them grippas." Slim said cutting Jig off.

"Yeah my nig. What type of mix is that? You know you could've hollered at me."

"On the real my nig, when I first answered my phone I thought you been on some other shit. Word! But yeah, I got a lil something-something. I was gonna get at you but it slipped my mind. I been duck off for the last couple of days."

"So, when can I holla at you?" Jig asked.

"I can stop by your spot in about 15 or 20 minutes. What you hittin' fo'?"

"How much you letting them go for?"

"I got you. I'll give you a thousand for three thousand."

"Bring me two thousand."

"Bet. I'll be there in a minute."

Soon as Slim hung up the phone with Jig, his phone started ringing again.

"Fuck!" he screamed in frustration. When he looked at the caller I.D. and saw that it was his Boo Thing, he started smiling and answered the call.

"Wussup baby girl? What's good with you?"

"Chilling looking at TV. You had me thinking about you all day yesterday."

"Oh yeah? What you been thinking about?"

"I'd rather show you then tell you. You coming to see me today?"

"Right now, I'm doing the father and son thing. I'm about to take lil man to the mall. I'll come through later after I'm finish chilling with him."

"Can I get something from the mall?"

"Not today baby. Me and my son doing our thing but I got you next time."

"I was just joking baby."

"Yeah right." Slim said sucking his teeth. "I'll holla at you later, baby. Now get off my line."

When they finally made it back home, he told Mann to go upstairs and change out his school clothes.

"We gotta meet Red and Baby K at the mall." Slim said. Mann ran to his room to change his clothes and Slim called Red.

"I was just about to call you. Me and Baby K walking out the door now." Red said.

"Type-a-thing. I'll see you in a minute."

Just as Slim was putting his phone in his pocket it started ringing again. It was Jig.

"Damn mix, I guess you forgot about me?" Jig asked.

"Boy, I glad you hit me back. I damn sure did forget. I'm coming right now."

"A'ight family. Mix!"

Jig was sitting on his porch smoking a blunt when Slim pulled up outside of his apartment. Slim got out of his car and went to sit on the porch next to Jig. He already knew Jig was gripping because of the way he been gritting his teeth. He put the pills on the porch between him and Jig.

"Damn my nigga. You gripping early today init?" Slim stated.

"You know I stay snatch family. Here, you want to hit this blunt?" Jig asked handing Slim the blunt. "Let me go grab the money off the table."

Jig went into the house and came back out and sat back down on the porch. He gave Slim the money and took the blunt back.

"I'll get at you later. I got to go meet Red and I got my lil man in the car." Slim said getting up to leave.

***

"Where you at? I'm parking now." Slim said pulling into one of the parking spaces closest to the food court side of the Northwoods Mall.

"We're inside of the Kids Footlocker. It took you long enough." Red replied.

"I had to stop and holla at Jig. We're coming in now."

When Slim walked into the Kids Footlocker, Red and Baby K were sitting on the bench and she was trying on a pair of the new Air Force l's mixed with Jordan's. Red saw Slim and stood up to give him dap. Then he gave Mann a dap.

"Hey Kaela." Mann said. "Daddy, I want a pair of those." he said pointing at Baby K's feet.

"Let me get a pair of this same pair in a size 3." Slim said to one of store clerks.

Red, Slim, Baby K, and Mann stopped at just about every kid store in the mall. After two hours of shopping, they went over to the food court to eat. Then Slim and Red allowed the kids to play in the play area while they watched and talked.

"I meant to tell you that Lisa is supposed to be going to ole girl wake today. Last time I talked to her, she was at Meka's people house on the Macon." Slim said.

"You talking about ole girl from the other night?" Red asked.

"Yeah. You know I played stupid and was like, 'ain't that the girl who got shot up with ole boy Trap?' and she was like, 'yeah that's her'. But guess what else my nig?"

"What?"

"That nigga ain't dead. The nigga been in a coma the whole time and he just came out that shit yesterday."

"What else she say?"

"That's really it, except that dawg all fucked up and we both already know that."

"He don't know it was us so fuck it."

"I feel the same way but we probably just need to fall back for a couple of weeks because you know Trap's brothers probably out there tryna see who's making hella moves."

"So, what you wanna to do? We can dip to Tennessee for a couple of weeks and go chill with my dawg Cool Hand. He already know we supposed to be coming through. We can leave at the end of the week."

Slim nodded and said, "Type-a-thing. I'll let Lisa know I got to shoot O.T. (out of town) for about a week. Go ahead and hit Cool Hand up and let him know what time it is."

"I can do that. You still taking your Boo Thing?"

"Off top. I'ma let her know what's up when I go see her tonight."

"Bet. I'll put Tiny on point when I get back to the house. You ready to slide out this mall?"

"Yeah, lets ride. You want to take the kids to Frankie's Fun Park? I don't think Lisa gonna be home until about 9 or 10 o'clock."

"Yeah we can do that. After we leave Frankie's we can take them to the movies."

"Aight, lets bounce then."

***

Slim and Mann didn't get home until after 11 p.m. Lisa was lying in bed reading another one of her books called, *Let That Be the Reason.*

She looked up from her book when Red entered the bedroom

and said, "It's about time ya'll got home. What did ya'll do today?"

"Mann, go get ready for bed. You got school tomorrow." Slim instructed. Once their son left the room, Slim said, "I took him shopping, we went to Frankie's Fun Park, then saw a movie. How long you been home?"

"I got in round 9:30."

"How was the wake?"

"It was sad, but they did a good job on her. She looked like she was sleeping."

"So, what they saying about ole boy Trap? He doing alright?"

"I really don't know too much about the situation. I just heard he came out of his coma yesterday and Meka brother said he was tortured."

"Damn. That's fucked up. I'm sorry to hear about your friend. I know Trap from around the way, so I hope he pulls through. I'm about to catch my cut. You know I ain't really did nothing since Sunday."

"Be careful and call me. I'll be up."

"A'ight. Oh yeah, before I forget, me and Red going out of town at the end of the week."

"How long ya'll planning on being out of town for?"

"I don't know yet, but I'll let you know what's up by the end of the week."

"Ok. I'll see you in the morning. Come give me a kiss before you go."

As Slim was walking out the door he remembered that he had to call Chedda.

"Damn zeek, I thought you done fake mix me." Chedda said when she answered her phone.

"Nah. Me and Mann been out and about all day. Where you at?" he asked.

"On the back street (Sumner Ave.) walking towards the Bottom (Read St.)."

"Meet me on Mole Lane by yourself. I'll be there in five minutes."

When Slim pulled up to the apartments on Mole Lane, a street over from the Bottom, Chedda jumped in his car. He handed her two sandwich bags which contained two ounces and a quarter spoon of coke. He told her that he wanted $2100 back and instructed her to call him when she was finish.

"Slim, you know I don't know how to cook this shit. Why you ain't give it to me already rocked up?"

"Chedda, I'm in a rush." he said sucking his teeth. "Come on. Let's go to Randy house."

When they got to Randy's spot nobody was in there because everybody was chilling outside. They went straight to the kitchen and grab the pyrex, baking soda and a bent-up fork from under the sink.

"Pay attention." Slim said as he grabbed Plat's clock from the cabinet. He placed a zone of white in the pyrex, then added 10 grams of baking soda to it. He filled half of the pyrex with water, then placed the pyrex in the microwave for 5 minutes. While he was waiting on the water to boil, he turned the hot and cold water on in the sink and waited until the water was at the right temperature. After 3 minutes, the water inside of the pyrex started to boil. Slim took the pyrex out the microwave and started sprinkling water from the facet in it. At the same time, he poured the water back out making sure the melted coke didn't pour out. When all the melted coke drop to the bottom of the pyrex glass, he poured almost all the water out the glass. He then took the fork and whip it a few times to stretch it a little. He hurried and placed more warm water in the pyrex, making sure to tap the glass against the counter a few times, so the dope didn't harden up.

"Why you did that?" Chedda asked.

"Sometimes that knocks the air bubbles outta the dope." he replied.

Slim let the pyrex sit for 5 minutes. Then he cut the hot water off and had only the cold water coming out the faucet. He took the pyrex and dipped it under the cold water. As the water in the pyrex turned cold, the cookie came loose and started floating in the pyrex. He let the cookie air dry for about 5 minutes then placed it on the clock. It weighed 33 grams.

"This is what you call slime ball bussa. The next best thing to straight drop." Slim boasted.

"You got to show me that again." Chedda stated.

"Gurl, you trippin! I already told you I been in a rush. I'll show you again tomorrow. If you don't learn tomorrow, then that's a rap. I'm charging you. The game is to be sold not told."

"Type-a-thing. Well, since you're in a rush, go head. I'll clean this up." Chedda told him.

"I already know you gonna clean up. I hope you ain't been expecting me to do it." he said walking off. "Be careful and call me when you ready to mix up."

Slim walked into Boo's house a little after one in the morning. She was in the bed looking at Sex in the City.

"I thought you wasn't coming. How was your day with your son?" she asked.

"Red and Kaela was with us, too. Them churn almost ran us crazy."

"So, I'm guessing you're tired?"

"Just a little bit, but I'm straight. You ready to show me what you been thinking about?" he asked smiling.

Thirty minutes later, after they got through having sex, Slim and Boo laid in bed cuddled up each other's arms.

"We leaving for Tennessee Friday or Saturday. You still want to go right?" Slim asked.

"Yeah, I still want to go. How long we gonna be gone?"

"I don't know yet. No longer than a week."

"Can you give me some money to leave with my momma and daughter while we're gone?"

"That ain't no problem. Let me get up and make a phone call before I go to sleep."

He left out of the room to call Lisa. He talked to her for about 10 minutes, then came back in the room and got back in the bed.

He and Boo watched TV until they both drifted off to sleep.

CHAPTER 9

"Yo." Slim answered the phone sounding irritated and sleepy.

"Rise and shine. Get up zeek. I'm on my way to the Mount." Red responded.

"I ain't on the Mount. I'm at Boo's spot."

"She lives in the Off Spree apartments, right?"

"Yeah, apartment B-5."

"I'll be there in 10 minutes. I'm getting off on Cosgrove now."

Slim ended the call with Red and nudged Boo. "Baby, get up. Red about to come over here."

"Maaaaan!" Boo whined, upset that Slim had woke her up. "He ain't coming to see me, he's coming to see you." Then she turned over and went back to sleep.

Slim curled his lip up at her and said, "Stink mouth." He then got up and went into the bathroom. By the time he had finished pissing and brushing his teeth, Red was knocking on the door.

"Wussup? Where Boo at?" Red asked as he entered the apartment.

"She's in the room sleeping."

"Well, let me holla at you in the car."

They walked outside and got in Red's car. Red sparked up the blunt he was smoking on his way there and passed it to Slim.

"I was thinking we should hit another lick before we dip. I was on D. Road last night hollering at Suga B.'s crazy ass in Evanston apartment when I saw C-Lo coming out of one of the apartments around there. Suga B. said C-Lo is fucking with a lil' broad that lives around there. She supposed to be pregnant by him too. Suga B. thinks they live together." Red said then hit the blunt.

"You think dawg gonna be slippin' after what happened to Trap and G-Money?"

"Slim, you know if we put the right pressure on him, he'll talk."

"Red, I know how you are, and I know how I am. I could care less about what we do to C-Lo, but I ain't tryna beast on no pregnant bitch. That's where I draw the line."

"Nigga, you just killed a bitch last week because she recognized you. Now you're sitting here worrying about a pregnant bitch? You gotta be shittin' me."

"The reason I killed that bitch is because she knew who I was. I'm not going down for no home invasion and all that other shit that comes with that. If she didn't know me, she would've still been alive today. Now suppose the same shit happens when we run up in this mix?"

"If the broad in there, I'll handle her. You can handle C-Lo. I ain't gonna pop her but I am gonna slap her ass around."

"Nigga, you already know I wasn't gonna say no to that. When is this shit going down?" Slim asked.

"Tomorrow night."

Red's phone started ringing. "Who calling me from your number?"

"Must be Boo, answer it."

Red answered the phone then passed it over to Slim.

"Wussup?"

"You want some breakfast?" Boo asked.

"Yeah. I'm right outside in the parking lot. I'm about to come back in."

"Ask Red if he's eating."

"Yeah he is. We coming in now."

"Oh and somebody has been blowing up your phone."

"Don't be answering or looking through my phone. You might see something you don't want to see."

"Boy, I don't even rock like that. Get off my line."

***

"You ready to get this lick?" Red asked when Slim answered his phone.

"I'm right ya waiting on you." Slim replied.

"Well, look out your door. I'm outside ho."

"I got yo ho, nigga. I'm coming right now." Slim said and then ended the called. He made his way down to the car and got in.

"I rode by C-Lo's spot before I came here. His car was parked out front. You feel like driving?" Red asked.

"Yeah, I'll drive." Slim got back out of the car and swapped places with Red. Once he was inside again, he said, "Lisa went to the funeral today."

"Forreal? I wonder if Tee-Tee and them were there."

"I don't know, I didn't ask. Feel me? What you got in here to listen to?"

"Man, this is a stollo. You better listen to Z.93."

When they pulled into Evanston apartment complex, Red pointed out C-Lo's car and said, "See his shit right there. Pull around back and park."

They both got out of the car and jogged up to C-Lo's door. They rolled their masks down over their faces then Red kicked the back door so hard that it came off its hinges.

"Goddamn nigga! Just wake up the whole damn neighborhood!" Slim whispered as they rushed into the apartment.

***

C-Lo's girlfriend was in the bedroom upstairs on the phone talking to one of her girlfriends when she thought she heard something fall downstairs.

"Let me call you back." she said and ended the call. She climbed off of the bed and went to see what caused the noise. As she started walking down the stairs, she saw two masked men running up the stairs towards her. She panicked and screamed before throwing her phone at them. She took off running back up the stairs and down the hall to her room.

***

Red saw the phone come at him and ducked just in time for it to go over his head. It ended up hitting Slim instead. Red left Slim behind and continued after her. He got to the door just as she was trying to lock it. He pushed his way inside and began tussling with her. They fell into the door, slamming it shut. Slim charged towards the door and fought to get into the room because he thought that Red was being attacked by C-Lo.

Red pushed the girl down on the bed and slapped her so hard he busted her lip. "Bitch! Where that nigga at?" he demanded.

"I don't know, I don't, I don't know! I'm pregnant, please don't hurt me. I swear I don't know where he is!" she cried.

"You think I give a fuck about you crying, bitch? You think this shit is a game? Where the dope and money at?" he asked and slapped her in the face again.

"I swear I don't know nothing! Please don't hurt me! Please ya'll, I'm pregnant! Oh God please don't hurt me or my unborn child! I'm begging you!"

"Bitch, you better not be lying." Red looked over his shoulder at Slim and said, "Search this muthafucka my nigga while I watch this bitch." he then looked down at her and said, "if he finds anything I'm gonna kill yo stupid ass and that fucking baby bitch!"

Slim left and started searching the second room that was up there. It was full of clothes and shoes, but nothing more. He went through the shoes on the floor one by one but came up empty. So, he went downstairs to search each room. The living room looked like a hurricane blew through it by the time he was done in there. After all of that, he still came up empty handed. Slim moved his search to the bathroom, the utility closet, and the kitchen. He looked inside of cereal boxes, the refrigerator, and the cabinets. Any place he thought someone would use as a hiding place was checked, yet he still didn't find anything.

"Man, ain't shit in the muthafucka." Slim said once he made it back up to the room where Red was.

"Bitch, where the fuck C-Lo stash at?" Red yelled while pointing his gun at her stomach.

"Please don't! I don't know where it is! I'm not lying, please don't hurt me and my baby!" The girl screamed.

Red punched her in the eye.

"My eye! My eye! Oh my God, my eye!" she cried.

"Watch this bitch while I search this room." Red told Slim.

Red searched the entire room and couldn't find anything. He went back over to the girl and said, "Bitch where C-Lo stash at? I know you know!"

"Please don't hurt me. I'm pregnant." she cried as she held her left eye. "Please let me go. I swear I don't know nothing."

"Bitch you think I give a fuck about you being pregnant? You got me fucked up! You better know where something at because we ain't leaving out of here empty handed. I should box your stupid ass right in the stomach." he said, and backhand slapped her across the face.

"Man, let's get the fuck outta here before somebody call the damn police about all of this noise this bitch is making." Slim said. He could see Red becoming out of control. He just wanted to get out of there.

"Fuck that! This bitch gonna tell us something or she coming with us!"

"Please, God help me! I swear I don't know nothing. Please just let me go. Please oh God please! I swear I don't know nothing!" she cried.

"Shut the fuck up bitch with all that noise. You praying to God when you need to be praying to me." Red said as he mushed the side of her head. "Watch this bitch while I search this house again. Something gotta be in here."

When Red left the room, the girl turned to Slim and asked him if she could go to the bathroom. She got up without waiting for a response.

"Get your ass back on the bed and don't fucking move." Slim demanded. He pointed his .44 at her and said, "If you want to use the bathroom, you better shit or piss right where you are."

The sight of his gun made her pee on herself. The more she pissed, the harder she cried.

"Why are ya'll doing this to me? I don't know nothing. I'm pregnant, don't you think if I had known anything I would've told ya'll by now. Please don't hurt me or my baby. I swear I don't know nothing!"

Slim got tired of the girl begging, plus he been ready to get the fuck up outta there. So, he said fuck it and walked out of the room to go find Red.

"Let's get the fuck outta here!" Slim said after finding Red in the kitchen.

"Why you leave that bitch upstairs by herself? Man, I told you to watch her."

"Dawg! Let's ride out. Ain't shit in here and you done beat the broad enough. If something was here she would've told us. I told you I ain't tryna beast on no pregnant broad so let's slide." Slim demanded.

Red looked at the slim for a second and said, "Fuck it, let's ride out."

***

Back in the house, the girl didn't know if they had left or not. She was too afraid to check, so she decided to climb out of the window instead. She walked across the roof and went to her neighbor's place. She tapped on the window, but no one came to the window. So she tried to climb down and jump off of the rood.

***

As Slim slowed to a stop at the exit of the apartment complex, Red tapped him on the shoulder and pointed out the window. Slim looked to see where Red was pointing at and they both stared at the girl as she tried to find a way down from the roof. They watched as she lost her balance and fell down hard landing on her stomach.

"Damn, you see that shit?" Red asked while laughing.

Slim just shook his head and drove off.

"Damn, Slim. I really thought that nigga been in the apartment. We might as well forget about zeek. You know that nigga about to be all the way on point now. We should've napped that bitch, for real. She knew exactly where that shit was at."

"Fuck that lick, bruh. I'm just glad we ain't get trap off in that mix. That bitch was in there screaming like a muthafucka."

"Did you see that broad fall? She hit the ground and just laid there." Red laughed.

"You'sa crazy ass dude ya kno." That broad probably lost her baby when she hit the ground."

"So! I don't give two fucks. Man, you know what...we should've checked the fucking car. Turn around!"

"Nigga, is you crazy? That's a dead mission. I'm about to carry my ass in the house and give my BM some dick." Slim said and turned down Remount road.

"I hope you done holla at everybody because we out this bitch tomorrow morning, so be up when I call you."

"Yeah, I done holla at my people. I even threw them something extra. The only thing I'm sitting on is a half of brick. I still got an ass of pills and some green but that's me and Lisa's personal stash. I ain't selling none of that." Slim said as she came to a stop outside of his house.

"Lisa fucked my head up when I saw her smoking the other day with Tiny. When we were in the house, her and Tiny been cheefing in the car. That's why Tiny ain't come in that night."

"She don't smoke like that, plus I don't be wanting her to mix around any and everybody. Did you get to handle your business with your people?"

"Off top. I even hollered at my nigga Crunch off of Liberty Park. I'm all about sitting just like you. I wish we had hit that lick though. We would've been sitting straight until we got back home."

"That shit is dead family. Ya can't cry over spilt milk, just charge it to the game. We can carry some bread and get right out there."

Red nodded and said, "That's wussup. Let's carry like forty a piece incase they're faking with those prices."

"Bet it up. I'ma head in, I'll holla at you in the a.m." Slim got out of the car and went inside the house. Lisa and Mann were asleep in the bed when he came into the bedroom. He picked Mann up and took him to his room.

"Wussup daddy?" Mann said sleepily. Slim laid him in the bed and tucked him under the covers.

"Wussup lil nigga. Go on back to sleep. I'll see you in the morning."

Slim went back to his bedroom, stripped out of his clothes, and slid into the bed next to Lisa. He noticed that she was wearing one of his t-shirts and a thong. She was lying in a position that made her ass sit up. He squeezed it then eased down to kiss her inner left thigh. When she didn't move, he trailed his kisses further down to her feet and back up. When his tongue slid over the fabric of her blue thong that sat on top of her clit, she moaned and opened her legs a little wider.

"Oh baby…that's my spot. Let me take this thong off." she moaned.

Slim was already in a zone. He was licking her pussy through her thong. All she could do was grab the back of his head and grind her hips to the rhythm of his tongue strokes until she came. After she got the first orgasm, he let her take her thong off and went back to sucking on her pussy.

"Oh God baby! That feels so good! Right there daddy! Oh right there! Eat my pussy! Damn you're eating this pussy good, I love you!" she moaned in ecstasy.

Slim held her pussy lips open with his thumb and forefinger as he continued teasing her clit with his tongue.

"Oh shit Slim, oh shit baby! What are you doing? I'm about to cum, don't stop! I'm coming!" she screamed as her legs and body started shaking. She held his head between her legs and near suffocated him.

"Turn over so I can hit that thing from the back." Slim instructed her while sucking her juices from his fingers. Her pussy was nice and wet when he slid his dick inside of her. He started off stroking her slow until he found his rhythm. Then he eased one of fingers inside of her ass. Being penetrated in both holes at the same time was driving her crazy. She started bucking and rocking back as she came for the third time.

"Let me get on top." she demanded, wanting to be in control.

They switched positions and for the next twenty minutes, she rode him frontwards, backwards, and sideways. Slim couldn't hold back any longer. With a loud roar, he bust off a nut inside of Lisa.

She pulled his still hard dick out of her and jacked the rest of his nut out of him. Getting off the bed, she went into the bathroom to retrieve a hot was rag. After wiping his dick off, she sucked him into another toe-curling nut.

Slim and Lisa laid in bed passing a blunt back and forth trying to recoup from the sex they just had while Erykah Badu's "Window Seat" played softly in the background.

"Me and Red leaving in a few hours to go to Tennessee." he said blowing a cloud of smoke into the air before passing the blunt to Lisa.

"You sure know how to fuck up a good mood...I'm just joking." Lisa said and kissed his chest. "When will ya'll be back?"

"We shouldn't be gone longer than a week."

"Baby just be careful. Every night I pray you make it in this house safe. So, I'm going to pray that you have a safe trip going and coming back."

"That's what I love about you. When it comes to me taking care of my business, you never complain. You always tell me to be careful."

"What am I supposed to do? Nag you? All that's going to do is make you stay away from home to avoid the confrontation. That's why some of these broads can't keep their man. They're always complaining about this and that. Baby, you're my man and I always got your back. You take care of me and our son. What more can a bitch ask for? I don't want you to think that I'm stupid or slow. I know you be dipping out on me from time to time, but you treat me like a queen. Your ass is slick too because I never catch you fucking off. That shows that you care about my feelings and I know how to play my position. If I ever do catch you slipping, I gonna be playing the position of a crazy baby mama and beat you and that bitch ass. I refuse to let another bitch have what's mine out in the open. I'm number one and you better make sure they know that. Like Tupac song say, 'you can run the street with your thugs, I'll be waiting on you.' I'll be right here baby when it's all over with."

"Baby, you should know I ain't going nowhere. No bitch can take your spot. If something were to happen to me, you and Mann gonna be straight. Believe that."

"Slim, you just don't know how much I love you."

"How much you love me?"

"Do you really want to know?"

"I ask didn't I?"

Lisa sat up so she could look him straight in the eyes. "I'll kill for you and over without thinking twice."

Slim could see just how serious she was. "Damn baby, that's deep."

"That ain't deep, that's real." she said.

"I'll bust a nigga head over you and Mann too. I love you and only death can stop that. Even then my spirit will still love you."

Slim and Lisa fell asleep in each other's arms after they finished their third blunt.

CHAPTER 10

Slim woke up to the smell of bacon and eggs. Lisa came up to the room to hand him his phone. She stood over him in a wife beater and a pair boy shorts the had red hearts all over them. Her feet were covered with a pair of fluffy house slippers.

"That's Red on the phone." She stated and rushed back to the kitchen. "Breakfast will be ready in ten minutes."

"Yo, wussup zeek?" Slim yarned into the phone and wiped the cold from his eyes. "What time is it?"

"Time to get your ass up! It's 10:40, nigga." Red responded.

"You done holla at that nigga Cool Hand?"

"I about to call him after I get off the phone with you. I had to give you a wakeup call first because you'll sleep all day if somebody let you."

"I'm getting up right now to get myself together. After I eat and pack a few things I'ma let Lisa drop me off. You tone mixxin right?"

"What kind of question is that? You know I'm taking my pistol. Man get off my line and don't forget to bring your check."

An hour later, Slim's money green colored Lincoln Towne car pulled up outside of Red's apartment. He got out of the car and grabbed his luggage from the back seat. Lisa told him to be careful and to call her soon as he got to Tennessee.

"Ain't you gonna get out and give me a hug and a kiss goodbye?" he asked.

"I'll give you a hug and a kiss, but not for a goodbye. When a person says bye sometimes that means forever. I'll see you later."

Red came outside just as Lisa was pulling off ready to crack jokes on Slim.

"I thought ya'll was about to rip each other clothes off and start fucking in the street. You got good timing. Tiny just called me and said her and your Boo Thing were on the way back here."

"You called ole boy yet?" Slim asked as they walked inside the apartment.

"Yeah. He told me to call him back because he just sat down

in the barber chair. That was thirty minutes ago. Let me call him back." Red said as he sat down on the couch and began dialing Cool Hand's line.

"Wussup Jones?" Cool Hand said when he answered his phone. "I see you're up early."

"What's good wit cha zeek? I'm up early because I'm tryna jump on this road and head your way."

"I thought that was a move for tomorrow."

"That's why I called you earlier to let you know that there's been a change in the plan. I hope I ain't killing the set."

"No, you ain't killin no set mane. Everything good."

"What's the best way to get there from here? Oh yeah our gals will be riding with us too."

"It's two ways to get here but the way I always take is I-20. You ride that all the way to Mississippi. Once you get in Tupelo, Mississippi get on 78 and that will run you into South Memphis. It's like an 11-hour ride. Call me once you get on 78. I'll meet you at this shake joint call Show Girl. What time are you riding out?"

"In about an hour, maybe an hour and a half. We should be there around 11 p.m., no later than midnight."

"That's good timing because I got to drop one of my bitches off to that shake joint around that time. Be careful on that road mane. Call me when ya'll get in Tupelo."

"A'ight pimpin'. I'll see you then." Red ended the call and let Slim know that everything was good to go.

"Call Tiny and see where the hell they at." Slim told him.

Just as Red started to dial Tiny's number, her and Boo came walking through the front door. Boo was wearing an off-white House of Dereon blouse and skintight House of Dereon jeans by Beyonce'. She was also wearing a pair of three-inch stiletto boots and Steve Madden shades. Tiny was rocking Apple Bottom blue denim jeans that showed off her pink thong. Her matching Apple Bottom mid length shirt displayed the 2-karat diamond ring on her belly button. On her feet were a pair of all white Air Force l's and she had on a pair of white D&G shades.

Boo walked up and gave Slim a kiss. The scent of her White Diamond perfume greeted him too. "You know I need to drop some money off to my momma or did you forget?" she asked.

"We'll take care of that before we ride out" Slim replied.

"You done handle everything?" Red asked Tiny.

"Yeah. Momma had something slick to say when I carried her the money earlier." Tiny replied.

"What her crazy ass had to say, and what kind of car you rented?"

"She called you a cheap red fucka."

Everybody started laughing.

Tiny continued, "We'll be riding in one of those new Lincoln MKS's."

"I gave that lady Five hundred dollars and let her use my car and she still got the nerve to call me cheap? Call her and tell her if we stay out of town over a week I'll Western Union her some more money. And tell her don't be in here eating all of our food with her ungrateful ass."

"A'ight." Tiny shook her head and began dialing her mom's line.

After leaving Boo's mother's house, they made a stop at Ihop to grab something to eat before they got on the road. Tiny and Boo were to take turns driving. Slim and Red didn't want to chance driving with the money, guns, and little bit of dope they had on them.

"Why they call your friend Cool Hand?" Boo asked making conversation.

"I've been wondering the same thing." Slim stated as he rolled a blunt.

"Dawg said he's a pimp and that's his pimp name." Red replied.

"He's a pimp? I ain't never met a real life pimp before. You sure that nigga ain't fakin?" Tiny asked.

"Girl, how you mean you ain't never met a pimp before? I'm one in the flesh." Slim joked.

"Nigga, you ain't no muthafuckin pimp." Tiny said sucking her teeth.

Everybody laughed.

Red grabbed the blunt from Slim and said, "I don't think dawg faking with that pimp shit. I used to look at dawg flicks when we been up the road. Zeek had a lil stable of ho's and he used to be on visit with three or four broads at a time. But I don't know why they call him Cool Hand. I never asked."

"Do he be wearing suits, gators, and got his hair all permed out and shit?" Boo asked.

"Girl this ain't the old days or the movies. That's why ya'll probably ain't never seen a pimp before. Ya'll be looking for them to look like the pimps from the old days. Zeek dress like everybody else. He had his shit permed out before he came to prison, but I don't know about now. On the real though, when we get to Memphis don't ya'll be acting like no kids at Disney World.

You all star struck and shit."

Boo turned around and said, "Let me ask you one more question."

"What Boo?" Red responded becoming irritated.

"Does he beat his girls? I mean I ain't tryna sit back and watch a nigga straight beat a bitch for no reason."

"Boo, you look at too much damn TV. I can't sit here and say if he beat his bitches or not, but if he do beat em' they probably deserve it."

When they got to Alabama Boo took over the wheel. Red and Slim were in the back seat smoking another blunt and rolling off the pills they had took when they were riding through Georgia. Tiny and Boo were up in the front seat smoking their own blunt.

"Ya'll two want to split a pill?" Red asked them.

"I'm straight. I ain't never popped them shits before." Boo answered

"I'll wait until we get where we're going. You know what them shits do to me." Tiny responded laughing.

It was 9:45 p.m. when made it to Tupelo, Mississippi. The

second they merged onto the 78, Red picked up his phone and dialed Cool Hand.

"What's up Mane? Where ya'll at?" Cool Hand asked.

"We just hopped on 78." Red told him.

"A'ight. I'll meet ya'll at the shake joint. Ya'll should be herr in another hour. Be careful in Mississippi. Dem red necks crazy round them parts. Call me once ya'll cross the border and see the sign that says welcome to Tennessee."

"A'ight family. Mix. " Red ended the call.

***

"Wussup zeek?" Red stated as he gave Cool Hand dap.

"What's up Mane? You kno tha sco, ten toes about my dough, and checkin a ho."

Slim, Boo, and Tiny were in the car watching the exchange between Red and Cool Hand. When both men started walking back towards the car, Slim, Boo and Tiny all got out of the car.

"Cool Hand, this is my right-hand man Slim. The one I used to always tell you about up the road." Then he moved over next to Tiny and said, "This my gal, Tiny, and that's Slim's lil one, Boo. Everybody, this is Cool Hand."

"Let's fall up in this herr shake joint and chop it up. I got a few of my hoes in there and they might start missing daddy. Feel me?" Cool Hand stated after they finished their greetings.

Cool Hand introduce two of his hoes to, Lee Lee and Tiffany, to everybody as they sat in one of the booths ordering drinks and talking.

"One of my girls work herr. I'll introduce ya'll to Key-Key later." he stated.

There was this one sexy young-looking female who kept coming to Cool Hand whispering something in his ear then leaving. She was light skin and stood at 5'3 with a nice round ass and decent size titties.

"Wussup with zeek?" Red asked, referring to the female who kept whispering to Cool Hand.

"Mane, that's Carla. She's a fresh turn out square bitch. I picked her up from the University. Bitch was checking a pimp and her curiosity got the best of her."

Red took a sip from his drink and said, "I feel that. My people want to know why they call you Cool Hand."

"My man Pretty Tree gave me that name. He said it's because I keep a steady hand and a cool demeanor. Plus, I got diamonds in my pinky nails." Cool Hand replied showing everybody his pinky fingers.

"Nigga you'sa fool. What if one of your nails broke?" Red asked.

"I'm good. If they break my bitches gonna buy me another one. Ye-ain- know?"

"I like this nigga." Slim stated.

"Check it, you don't mind us camping out at your spot tonight, do you? We'll get ourselves a room tomorrow." Red asked.

"I'm Cool Hand, baby. You know I'm cool with that. Ya'll can camp as long as ya'll want. You don't have to get no room."

"I appreciate that." Red said. "But, I like to have my own space. I like to walk around in my boxers and sometimes naked."

Cool Hand said, "Tomorrow I'm taking you and Slim through North Memphis where I grew up at. We'll let the girls go shopping or something. Ya'll cool with that?"

"Well let's ride because we been on the road all day and we tired as a bitch." Red spoke up for everyone.

"Come on. We can bounce. I'll just have Lee Lee and Tiffany come back to pick up Key-Key and Carla."

Cool Hand lived in a house in an area known as Germantown. A suburb on the out skirts of Memphis.

"Damn dawg, you and your broads living good." Red said when he got out of the car.

"Don't none of my bitches live herr. This my shit playa. I like my space just like you. Lee Lee and Tiffany got their own crib in Klondike. They got to stay close to the Ave. (the ho stroll). Key Key live over in tha Bay. You know the area that Frayser Boy, from 3-6 Mafia, be talking about? Carla stay with Key Key right now cause Key Key getting her right. Key Key is my bottom bitch. That's the one who rode the whole bid out with me when those other broads started falling off. Come on ya'll, let's go in" He then turned to his ladies and said, "Lee Lee and Tiffany, ya'll hoes go back to the Shake Joint and wait on Key Key and Carla."

Cool Hand gave the keys to his red Cadillac SUV to Tiffany. Tiny and Boo were looking at Cool Hand and wondering, *who this lil nigga think he is?*

"I might have to switch the game up and started pimpin' myself if that pimp money got you living like this." Slim stated. "Shit, Cool Hand you might have to pull my coat to this pimpin' shit."

"Mane, the game is to be sold not told. Ye-ain-know?"

Everybody bust out laughing as they walked into Cool Hand's

house.

CHAPTER 11

Trap was sitting in his bed looking at TV and eating a bowl of jello when Tee Tee, Slugga, and C-Lo walked in. They had just left the 7th floor from visiting Tammy, C-Lo's girlfriend.

"Wussup ya'll, why the long faces?" Trapped asked after noticing everyone's long faces. "Damn C-Lo if you had miss me that much you should've been come by to visit me. You ain't gotta get all teary eyed and shit."

Trap tried to make a joke out of his situation to lighten the mood, but nobody was laughing.

"Are ya'll gonna tell me what's going on or do I have to lay here and guess?" he asked becoming frustrated.

"Lil bruh, we been here all morning. Two niggas kicked in C-Lo's gal's door last night and beat her up bad. Probably them same niggas who run up in your shit." Tee Tee spoke up.

"I know you're bulshittin'. You got to be kidding me! She

151

a'ight?" Trap asked.

"She lost my seed." C-Lo replied with tears rolling down his face.

"She fell off the roof tryna get away." Slugga stated.

"She fell off the roof!?" Trap was in disbelief.

"That ain't all that's happened since you been in here." Tee-Tee said.

"What else done happen?" Trap asked, still shocked by the news he just heard about C-Lo's gal.

"G. got killed Saturday. I was gonna tell you when I found out but at the time, you were going through it about Meka's death."

"What the fuck this is, bad news day? I don't care what I been going through. G. is my nigga, you should've told me that shit asap. Damn my nigga gone. Where they get my dawg at Tee-Tee?" Trapped asked.

"They caught him slippin at the stash house in West Ashley. Split my dawg wig wide open. Man, this shit crazy. First you, then G-Money, now C-Lo. Ain't no telling what would've happened if C-Lo had been there. I don't know what the fuck is going on but whoever it is, they're gunning for us."

"Ya'll mean to tell me that ya'll ain't heard nothing yet?" Trap screwed up his face. He couldn't believe that after all he'd learn, no one had any information to give about the niggas who killed his people. "Did they get anything?"

"Did they?" Slugga repeated the question angrily. "Hell yeah, they got something! They got two castles, a mansion, a hut, and a bag of sunflower seeds (two bricks of coke, one brick of heroin, a pound of weed, and ecstasy). And about 250 grand."

"Fuck man! They killin' us!" Trap said. "I'm sorry about what happen to your gal C-Lo, but did they get anything from there?"

"No. I don't keep nothing there." C-Lo responded.

"Good because whoever these niggas are, they killin' us. Real talk! I got to get the hell outta here. Somebody got to know something."

"We were on some lay back shit tryna see if we would hear anything." Slugga said looking at Tee-Tee. "But we about to find out what's really going on."

"I want to know who's responsible for this shit asap. If nobody wanna talk, make em. Matter of fact, I don't even feel like talking no more." Trap was so mad about everything he'd just heard he forgot to ask about his kids and Meka's funeral before everybody left.

After leaving the hospital, Tee-Tee, Slugga, and C-Lo was sitting in one of their trap spots in some apartments on South Rhett avenue talking about how they were going to put a handle on their situation.

"We ain't got nothing to really go on. These niggas ain't no ghosts. Somebody gotta know something. Let's ride through a couple of hoods and ask the people we know if they've heard anything about somebody having hella work out the blue, or suddenly spending hella money." Tee Tee said.

"Fuck that! I rather ride through every hood and snatch one or two of them lil niggas off the block and slap they lil ass up until they tell something. We can snatch junkies too for all I care." Slugga said.

"That's what I'm talking about." C-Lo stated shaking his head up and down. He was ready to take his anger out on anybody.

"If we move like that, we'll be putting them niggas on point to who is doing this and then they might try to go into hiding. If they do, we'll never find them. Slugga, stop being so damn amp! You and C-Lo talking so crazy ya'll ain't even thinking straight." Tee - Tee said.

C-Lo stood up and said, "Well, let's hit D-road first because there ain't nothing but a couple of people, outside of ya'll, who knew where my gal stayed at."

"Let's ride then." Slugga said grabbing his keys.

***

"Did you hear about the that break-in that happened last night in Evanston Apartments?" Detective Cummbee asked Detective Deckerd when they walked into their office.

"Where a female supposedly fell off the roof and lost her baby? Yeah, I heard about that." Detective Deckerd replied taking a seat.

"Guess who her baby father is?"

"I don't know, but I bet you're gonna tell me." Deckard stated.

"Carlos Smalls, Travis Green's cousin. That guy who got himself killed in West Ashley name was Gregory Ramsey. All these guys hung together."

"How in hell you know all this shit?"

"I'm a detective. Give me some credit. Plus, I got my sources. Something got to be going on because it looks like somebody is pissed off at these guys and trying to take the whole crew out."

Cummbee had Deckard's attention now.

"Let's get back to the hospital and have another talk with Mr. Travis Green and while we're there, we might as well have a talk with Mr. Smalls' girlfriend, too." Deckard suggested.

When both detectives entered Trap's room, he was laying in his bed staring up at the ceiling.

"How are you doing Mr. Green?" Detective Deckerd asked.

"Man, what the fuck ya'll want?" Trap asked snapping out of his trance.

"Oh, now you can talk." Detective Cummbee taunted.

"Man, I said what the fuck ya'll want!?" Trap asked again becoming agitated.

"We just wanted to ask you a few more questions. That's all." Detective Deckerd answered.

"You can ask me whatever you want, but that don't mean I got to answer."

"You're right. So, just answer what you want." Detective Deckard agreed. "Alright, let's try this again by starting with you. What really happened at your apartment the night you were shot? Do you know who killed Ta'Meka Washington or tried to kill you?"

"Last time ya'll were here, you and ole boy over there," Trap nodded over at Detective Cummbee. "had everything mapped out. So, why don't ya'll tell me what's going on since ya'll are the detectives."

"Mr. Green, we're trying to help you but how can we help if you're not willing to helping us?" Detective Deckerd asked.

"Listen to me man! I Don't Know Shit!!"

"Can I have a word with him now?" Detective Cummbee asked.

"Go ahead because I've tried to be reasonable with him."

"Trap, you don't mind if I call you Trap, do you? No, you don't mind." Detective Cummbee said answering his own question. "This is what we got so far. First, somebody kicks in your door, torched your little dick, shoot you three times, and leaves you for dead. Let's not forget that Ta'Meka Washington was killed in the midst of this. I'm positive it was a robbery/home invasion. Second, a man named Gregory Ramsey, who is also known as G-Money, was killed in West Ashley a few days later. From my understanding it was a robbery, home invasion, and homicide. However, I don't have all the specifics on that. Lastly, Tammy Boyd, the girlfriend of Carlos Smalls who goes by C-Lo, house was broken into last night and she lost the baby she was carrying. I'm willing to put my badge on it that it was also a home invasion. So, I must ask you, how do you like my detective skills Trap?"

"First off, only my friends call me Trap and you ain't no friend of mine. Second, what do all of these people have to do with me?"

"They got a lot to do with you, Trap. Carlos Smalls is your cousin and we also know that Gregory Ramsey was a close friend of yours. Do you want to talk to us now?"

"Like I said before, I don't know nothing."

"Suit yourself. I just hope nobody else dies because of your code to the streets. Let's get outta here." Detective Cummbee said to Detective Deckerd.

***

Detective Cummbee and Deckerd had decided to pay a visit to Tammy Boyd after an unsuccessful conversation with Trap.

"How are you Ms. Boyd? I'm Detective Cummbee and this is my partner Detective Deckerd. We would like to ask you a few questions."

"The police was here this morning and I already answered a lot of questions." she said in a weak voice.

"As you can see Ms. Boyd, we're not policemen, we are detectives and we promise to make this as quick as possible. Could you please tell my partner and I what you told the officers this morning?"

"I was in my room talking on the phone when I heard something fall downstairs. I went to go look and two people with masks on came running up the stairs. I tried run to my room, but one of them grabbed me. We tussled then I was hit hard and held down. One of them instructed the other to tie me up. While the other guy was gone, the guy that was holding me started feeling on me. I grabbed the lamp off the nightstand by the bed and hit him with it. Once I got myself free from him, I ran to the window. I climbed out onto the roof to get away, but I slipped and fell. They were going to rape me." she shook her head. "I lost my baby." she said as she started crying.

"You said there were only two people?" Detective Cummbee asked.

"Yes sir. That's all I saw." she answered.

"Thank you, ma'am. We're sorry that you lost your baby. We'll do our best to catch the people responsible for this. We'll let you get your rest now. If there's anything else you think of, feel free to give us a call anytime." Detective Cummbee said as he handed her one of his cards.

Both detectives wished Ta'Meka well and left.

"What do you think?" Detective Deckerd asked as they headed for the elevator.

"She's lying. The only truth in her story was the two masked men."

"And the fact that she fell off the roof and lost her baby."

"Yeah, that too."

***

After making their rounds to each hood on Dorchester road, Slugga, Tee-Tee and C-Lo stopped by the mall to pick up something to wear to G-Money's funeral. When they left the mall, they headed back to the South Rhett apartments to get in their own cars. They decided to meet up later and ride through a couple more hoods.

Later that night around 10:30 p.m. they all met back up outside of the apartments on South Rhett and hop into a van Slugga rented from a junkie. They rode through Union heights, Accabee and the Macon asking about the robberies and murders, but no one claimed to know anything. Slugga wanted to keep going but it was almost two in the morning.

Tee-Tee reminded him that they needed to be up and ready for G-Money's funeral the next day.

"We can hit the streets after we lay our dude to rest."

"After that, we hittin' the streets hard. Somebody knows something and I won't stop until I find out who is responsible for this shit." Slugga said agreeing to pause the search for the night.

CHAPTER 12

The following day, Key-Key and Carla showed up to Cool Hand's house to pick up Tiny and Boo. Key-Key stood at 5'5 and was slightly bowlegged. She had her cut short hair in a style similar to Halle Berry's. She also had hazel contacts in her eyes to compliment her high yellow skin complexion. The jet-black True Religion jeans she wore hugged her hips and ass perfectly. Key-Key was what you would consider a brick house. Carla was also looking flawless in her Apple Bottom one-piece outfit.

Boo and Tiny were dressed to the nines as well. Boo rocked a grey colored Gucci skirt set with a pair of matching Gucci sandals and Tiny sported a white and pink colored Dolce and Gabanna skirt set with white D&G sandals and a pair of white D&G shades.

After the women greeted each other with compliments and praises over their outfits, they all headed out to go shopping at the mall leaving the men to themselves.

"What ya'll wanna get into today?" Cool Hand asked Red and

Slim.

"It's whatever with me. I just want to see what's going on in the M-Town, zeek." Red replied.

"Yeah, let's see what's up with that North. You know that's what we call North Charleston." Slim said holding his thumbs up.

"We can do that playas but I'ma give ya'll a tour of the whole M-Town. It's more to Memphis then North Memphis." Cool Hand stated.

They all piled up in Cool Hand's Caddy truck and began their tour of downtown Memphis. They rode through Beale street and Cool Hand pointed out the sites as he told them about its history. Then he took them over to Stax Records, where some of the most legendary artists recorded their hits.

"See, all ya'll know about Memphis is the Three 6 Mafia's, Playa Fly's, and Yo Gotti's but this is where it all started. I'm talking about Issac Hayes, B.B. King, Al "Grits" Green, and Willie Hutch. Know what I'm talking about? Memphis 10, the city of the blues. That was when pimpin' was pimpin'. Ya dig?"

Cruising through South Memphis, Cool Hand pointed out Graceland, Elvis Pressley's estate and he also pointed out the historic home of Memphis Slim.

"Who's Memphis Slim?" Slim asked.

"That's the greatest pimp to ever walk the Memphis streets." Cool Hand answered.

On Poplar and Ayers street, Cool Hand pulled up to a residence that looked like a prison because of its big gray cinder block styled building and the tall fence that surrounded it. Cool hand got out of the car and motioned for Red and Slim to follow.

"This is the infamous Dixie Homes. This is where my daddy, Ed Lover, was raised and the apartments that my granddaddy, Sweet Willie Jones, was the landlord of and used to pimp out of. God bless the dead."

At that moment, four little boys spotted Cool Hand and ran up to him.

"Cool Hand! Cool Hand! I made the A/B honor roll!" Said one little boy.

"Cool Hand, I got two A's!" Said another.

Cool Hand smiled and said, "Well, since you made the honor roll here's $20 dollars and since you made two A's here's $10 dollars for you."

Another kid said, "Me and my brother only made B's. I know you said we gotta make A's, but we tried."

"Since you tried here's $5 dollars apiece. But I'm not gonna be so cool next time. Ya here."

"Thank you, Cool Hand. Cool Hand when I grow up I wanna be just like you." One of the boys told him.

"You don't wanna be like me baby boy. You wanna be greater than me. Now ya'll stick to your books."

Once the kids ran off, Slim said, "I like the way you show them lil niggas in the hood love. That's some real shit right there."

" Mane, ya gotta keep these lil chaps motivated, dig? I keeps it funky for the hood. Ye-ain-know. What ya'll Chuck Town niggas know about that promethazine? That purple drink?" Cool Hand asked.

"I don't know shit about it. I ain't never drink that shit before, zeek." Red answered.

"I drunk it one time. That shit had me real fucked up." Slim stated.

"Since Slim been so anxious to hit that North, we about to roll to Ridge Crest. The Crest is what we call it. That's where Yo Gotti be at. If he ain't on the road we might run into him."

When they pulled up to The Crest and got out of the truck, Red was excited. He was looking forward to seeing Yo Gotti because that was one of his favorite rappers. As they walked through The Crest, everyone showed Cool Hand love.

Cool Hand walked up to a guy he called John-John. They exchange a few words, then John-John began heading towards one of the apartments. Just before he disappeared beyond the doors, Cool Hand yelled out to him.

"Don't bring me no K-Roll neither. I want that thick shit, so when it hit the soda it be like it's about to explode."

"Mane, you know I ain't gonna play you like that Cool." John-John replied and kept walking.

He returned ten minutes later with three pints of syrup and gave it to Cool Hand. Cool Hand paid him then asked him if Yo Gotti was around.

"Mane, you know Gotti stay on the road doing his thing." John-John replied.

"Tell him to holla at a playa when he touchdown."

"A'ight. I got ya Cool. Be easy playa."

"Damn, I had want to meet that nigga." Red said as he got in the truck.

"Playa, me and Yo Gotti go way back, dig. If you don't see him before you go back to the Chuck I can always call you and let ya'll chop it up."

"Shit! Speaking of phone. I got to call my baby mother." Slim stated pulling out his phone.

"I need to make a quick run through Klondike." Cool Hand stated before pulling off.

"This yo' town. We riding with you." Red said as pushed his seat back.

Before they got to Klondike, they made a quick stop to a corner store to get a 2-liter of Sprite, two boxes of blunts, a pack of cigarettes, and three Styrofoam cups filled with ice. Slim also bought one hundred dollars' worth of scratch offs.

"I got some E pills." Red said to Cool Hand when they were back in the truck.

"Mane, I don't fuck with them pills playa. If it ain't green or purple I don't want it" Cool Hand replied mixing everyone's drink.

"More for me and Slim then. Nigga ye-ain-know!" Red said laughing.

"Mane, your ass still crazy." he said passing Red and Slim their drinks.

"Roll me up a stick, Jones. And don't put no white on my green." Cool Hand told Red.

They rolled through a neighborhood, known as Evergreen, on their route to Klondike.

"This is where Project Pat and Juicy J are from." Cool Hand pointed out. "On the cool, Big Pat sa'pose to be having some kind of special event at Club Liquid tonight. All the ladies get in free if they're wearing a red thong."

"Zeek, that's what's up. That shit sound exclusive." Red slurred. He was beginning to feel the effects of his drink.

"I ain't tryna mix with Boo and Tiny at no club. I tryna mix one of these broads from Memphis. Real talk, zeek!" Slim said, also slurring.

"Don't worry about that playa. I'll have my ho's take them to Pressure World in Orange Mound."

"Ain't that's where 8-Ball and MJG from? Them my fuckin niggas right there. I be on that 8-Ball and MJG shit. I grew up off them boy shit." Slim said then he started rapping one of their songs. "Lay it down, lay it down, you ho's lay it down."

"Yeah that's the Orange Mound. But my favorite cuts by them were *Pimps* and *Break a Bitch College*." Cool Hand said popping in a screwed and chop 8-Ball and MJG CD. He chose the song *Space Age Pimpin'*, turned the volume up and started rapping along to the lyrics.

"I know that's right!" Red said bobbing his head.

"Nigga ye-ain-know!"

When they finally got to Klondike, Cool Hand didn't even stop. He just rolled down Vollentine avenue checking to see if his hos were doing what they supposed to be doing. Seeing that they were, he kept on riding and they went back to Germantown.

Just as they pulled back up to Cool Hand's house, Red's phone rung. The caller ID showed that it was from Charleston, but Red didn't recognize the number.

"Who this is?" Red he answered.

"Wussup my nigga. This Suga B."

"Oh. Wussup zeek?"

"Boy, either you'sa crazy ass nigga or I don't know what I'm talking about."

"Nigga, what is you talking about?"

"Somebody run up in C-Lo's gal spot. That crazy bitch fall off the roof and lose her baby. I heard she took an ass cuttin too. C-Lo been round this bitch actin'. You know what I'm talking about?"

"Dawg, you off the chain. I don't know what the fuck you talking about."

"Tell me anything. But you and I both know you know I know what time it is. Last thing you got to worry about is me saying something. Anyway, C-Lo, Tee-Tee, and Slugga been round this bitch trippin and asking questions. Feel me?"

"Bruh, I ain't even in the Chuck. I'm out of town with my peoples. Feel me? I don't know what you talking about. Now get off my line. I'll holla at you when I get back in the Chuck."

"Bet it up."

"Who that been?" Slim asked.

"Suga B from D-road. He called talking about ole girl lose her lil one. Plus, he got a feeling that I hit up ole boy spot. You already know I told dawg I ain know what he talking about."

"You think he gonna say something?" Slim asked. "You know how niggas run their mouth when they think they know something."

"Naw. Dawg concrete solid. But to be on the safe side, I ain't admitting to nothing over no phone."

"I feel ya dawg. I 'm just tryna make sure that dawg ain't one of them niggas who got diarrhea of the mouth. I know of dawg, but I don't *know* dawg like that."

"Red, you know Cool Hand minds his own business, but the way ya'll two talking in front of me, I might as well be in ya'll's business. What's good playa?" Cool Hand asked.

At this time, they all were sitting in Cool Hand's living room nursing their third cup of syrup and taking a blunt to the head. The room was clouded with boonk and loud smoke.

"You already knew what my plans were before I got out. Right?" Red answered after blowing smoke out his mouth.

"I remember you back there stressin' over some gorilla shit."

Red told Cool Hand almost everything that happened back in Charleston leading up to the day they called and showed up in Memphis. He left out the part about them shooting Trap and killing the girl that was with him. He also didn't say anything about them killing G-Money or that a girl lost her baby during one of their robberies. Some things just aren't meant to share with everybody, no matter the reason.

"Damn Jones. You and Slim been busy as hell out there in the Chuck. Ya'll can lay low as long as you need to. As a matter of fact, ya'll don't got to get no hotel. If you want to walk around this bitch in your boxers, do you. But on the cool, we need to hit this mall before we get too fucked up. By the time we get back Key-Key and them should be here."

Later that night, everybody went out to California Dreaming for dinner. After they finished eating, they went their separate ways. The girls went to Key-Key house to get dressed for a night out at Pressure World. The guys headed to Cool Hand's house to get dress for Club Liquid.

They all walked into the club dressed to impress. Slim wore a True Religion black jeans suit with the hat to match, a V-neck white t-shirt, a pair of crispy white Air Force l's, and his long gold chain with the C.T.0 medallion. He also had on a pair of all black Ray Ban light tint shades.

Red was sporting white Robin jeans with the red trimming and red rhinestones on the back pockets, a white Robin t-shirt with the red writing on it, a red and white Red Sox fitted hat, and a pair of all red suede Air Force l's. On his eyes he wore Gucci red frame shades. His C.T.0 chain was also swinging from his neck.

Cool Hand was pimped out in a cream-colored Stacy Adams outfit with cream Stacy Adams shoes to match. He wore a ring on every finger except his thumbs. He had a Rolex watch on his left arm, and a Cuban link gold chain, with an iced out Jesus, on his neck.

Females and niggas were checking out the two new faces that were walking with Cool Hand. They could tell just by looking at Red and Slim's swag that they weren't from around there.

"Playas, we ain't even in the club yet and these ho's already choosing." Cool Hand stated.

"They ain't by themselves because I'm choosing too." Slim said winking at a short brown skin female with a mouthful of gold teeth.

The club was jam packed when they got inside. Females were walking around with little to nothing on. Almost every female had on red thongs. On their way to the bar, they noticed a few guys on the dance floor gangsta walking.

"Damn Cool, you ain't tell me a bunch of Crips would be in this mix. You know how I get down and I ain't got my ratchet on me." Red said, reminding Cool Hand of his affiliation. While in prison, Red paid his dues and became a blood.

"Where you see Crips at?" Cool Hand asked.

"See all them boy around them couple of fellas?" Red said pointing at the dance floor.

"Mane, them niggas ain't no Crips. We call that Memphis walkin'. Stop being so paranoid. Cool Hand won't put you in no fucked up predicament."

"I stay on point when it comes to my life." Red stated.

"Bruh, you already know I sneak my ratchet in this mix. I ain't know why you left your shit in the car. You need me to go get it and you hold mine?" Slim whispered in Red's ear.

"I ain't know how you did it, but yeah go snatch mine for me." Red answered.

"Let's go to the bathroom so you can get mine and tell Cool to give you the keys to the car."

It took Slim thirty minutes to go to the car and come back with Red's pistol. With their pistols on them they both felt safe and started drinking and mingling with the females. The females were loving the way Slim and Red talked. Some of them thought they were from the island due to the their Geechee accents. Being out of towners with a different swag and an interesting accent gave them a lot of leverage with the ladies. They probably could've left with any female they wanted to.

Three-Six Mafia and Project Pat did their thing on the stage. After their set, the group invited Cool Hand, Red and Slim to come and kick it with them for a while. Red and Slim chopped it up with the group and then turned their attention to the fine ass females that were in the room.

They ended up leaving the club early with three freaks and headed to grab breakfast and a hotel room. Red had a broad that looked a little like Gabrielle Union in the face, but she had a body like Buffy The Body. The broad that Slim had on his arm looked like Christina Milian. That's who he thought she was when he hollered at her in the club. Cool Hand had a light skin thick red bone that had that Beyonce' thing going on.

After they ate breakfast, they rented rooms at the Quality Suites. While on the elevator, Slim pulled out a bag of E-pills. He gave Red two pills and put two pills in his mouth washing it down with the bottle of water he had in his hand. He then passed the bottle to Red.

The women eyes lit up when they saw the bag of pills. The Christina Milian look alike asked as she could have one and Slim ended up giving all of them a pill. They passed the water bottle around, taking a sip to help wash the pill down. The elevator finally reached their floor and everyone got off and went their separate ways.

As soon as Slim shut the door to his room, he started coming out of his clothes. Either he was already high, or the pills had an instant effect on him. He dove onto the bed with his boxers, tank top, and socks on. The girl he nicknamed Christina, hopped on the bed with him and pulled his dick out through the hole in his boxers and started sucking his dick. She was sucking his dick like a porno star. She pulled off his boxers while he took off his tank top. Then she started sucking his dick again while massaging his balls at the same time. She was driving him crazy. She had his balls in her mouth while she stroked his dick. Slim moaned like a female as she took him to la-la land. He closed his eyes and tilt his head back. He could feel himself getting closer to his nut. Everything was going well until he felt her wet tongue slide across his asshole.

"Hold up zeek! I don't get down like that babe!"

She laughed, stood up, and began taking off her clothes piece by piece, like she was putting on a strip show. Slim couldn't take his eyes off her flawless body.

"What you gonna do Geechee boy, stare at me or give me some of that big dick?" she moaned as she massaged her clit and breast at the same time.

Snapping out of his trance, Slim got up and grabbed a condom out of the pocket of his crumpled up pants. Christina took the condom from him and put the tip of it between her teeth. Then she rolled it down over his dick with her mouth. She smiled as she climbed on top of him and eased down on his dick. Slim held onto her waist as she began riding him cowgirl style.

"Oh shit! Damn boy you got that good dick!" she moaned as she bounced up and down on him.

***

Red had the girl he was with positioned in the doggy style smacking the hell out of her ass as she kept begging him smack her ass harder.

"Oh, Gawd! I love it daddy! Beat me daddy! I been a bad girl!" she moaned.

Red was trying to keep up because she was throwing the pussy at him all kind of ways.

"Smack my ass harder, nigga! Smack it harder!" she demanded. The pill had her coming over back to back.

Red stuck two fingers in his mouth to get them wet and slippery with his spit. Then he rammed them in her asshole. She let out a loud moan and came again. Now that he was penetrating both of her holes, he he had her body under his control.

"I want it in my ass! Put it in my ass!" she demanded.

Red didn't have to be told twice. He pulled his dick out of her pussy and eased it into her ass slowly until he was halfway in. He started with slow short strokes, then he started long dicking her like he was trying to knock the sparks out of her ass. Red switched back and forth with fucking her in the ass and then in the pussy until he came. That explosion was so big that it weakened him, and he just fell back into the bed. Breathing heavy and feeling like the room was spinning, he said, "Damn you'sa nasty bitch."

***

Cool Hand was in his room getting slow head. He wasn't trying to fuck the broad he was with. He was plotting on putting the three females on his team. If not all, at least one of them.

***

It was after 5 a.m. when they made it back to Cool Hand's house. The ladies were out back chilling by the pool talking and smoking weed. Cool Hand's main bitch Key-Key had a key to his place and had let them in once they had returned from their night out. They stopped talking when they noticed that the men were back.

"Did ya'll have fun at the club tonight?" Tiny asked sarcastically.

"Yeah." Red answered in the same tone.

"Pressure World was off the chain. We even saw, um... What's that rapper name, Key-Key?" Boo asked.

"She talking about 8-Ball." Key-Key answered.

"Yeah, yeah, that's his name." Boo nodded.

"Well, we saw Three-Six and nem. We even chilled with them boy for a lil while up in V.I.P." Slim bragged.

Nobody was tired, so they partied until they started dropping out one by one.

CHAPTER 13

It was a hot afternoon and Slugga was by himself riding through the Mount in his black Impala sitting on 24-inch Hang Tyme rims. He was riding down Sumner avenue on his way to the four way listening to Rick Ross's *Everyday I'm Hustlin* track when he noticed someone trying to flag him down. At first, he didn't recognize who it was, but as he got closer, he realized it was his homie Lil Kris. Slugga pulled into the parking lot of a small apartment complex on the side of the road.

"Wussup lil nigga?" Slugga asked when Lil Kris stuck his head in through the passenger side window.

"You straight zeek? Cause my people ain't mixxin right now."

"Yeah I'm straight. What you tryna get?"

"How much you'll sell me a zone and a half for zeek?"

"I'll let you get that ming for the low. You either can ride with me to get it or give me twenty minutes to go get it."

"I don't want no soft."

"It's however you want it my nig. You riding or what?"

"Yeah, let's ride zeek." Lil Kris said and hopped in the car.

While they were riding, Slugga turned his stereo down and asked Lil Kris who he be getting his work from.

"I be fucking with my cousin baby daddy." he answered not knowing he was being investigated.

"Who? You talking about Slim?"

"Yeah, him and Red hella mixxin."

"Who's Red?"

"I don't really know dawg like that but he off the Mount. He just come home about ten months ago off a big boy bid."

"So that's who everybody be getting their work from round ya?"

"Damn zeek, you asking me a lot of questions. You questioning me like you the police or something. Nigga is you wired up?" Lil Kris asked in a joking manner.

"Nigga! Do I look like some fucking police? Who the fuck you playing with bitch ass nigga?" Slugga asked slamming on his breaks.

"Chill with all that bitch ass nigga shit nigga. I been just joking with you fool."

"Naw nigga, fuck that! Since you want to play, give me everything out your pockets bitch ass nigga and I ain't playing." Slugga demanded pulling his gun out and pointing it at Lil Kris.

"Man, Slugga I know you bullshitting. I know you ain't about to play me like this. Dawg you major." Lil Kris pleaded nervously.

Slugga knocked Lil Kris on the forehead with his pistol leaving a gash above his right eye.

"Think it's a game, nigga? Don't make me ask you a-fuckin-gain! Empty ya pockets before I air your ass out!" he said through clench teeth.

Seeing that Slugga was serious, Lil Kris didn't have to be asked no more. He gave up everything he had in his pockets as fast as he could.

"Now get the fuck out my car and walk ya lil punk ass back to the Mount!"

Riding off, Slugga had to laugh to himself because he really didn't mean to rob Lil Kris. He just spazzed out when Lil Kris called him the police. Plus, he took his anger out on him. He had a feeling it was Slim and Red breaking them off. He just felt it in his heart and he was right. He picked up his phone and dialed Tee-Tee's line.

"Wussup lil bruh?" Tee-Tee answered.

"Where you at zeek?" Slugga asked.

"South Rhett. Why, wussup?" Tee-Tee responded.

"I'm on my way there. I'll be there in ten. And I know who been hitting us." he said before he hung up.

"Where C-Lo at?" Slugga asked once he met up with Tee-Tee.

"I just got off the phone with him. He posted with Tammy; he'll be through later. But put me on point. What tha mix is?"

"You know Lisa, who live on the Mount babydaddy, Slim?" Slugga asked while lighting up a cigarette then offering Tee-Tee one.

"Yeah I know Slim off the Mount." Tee Tee answered taking the cigarette.

"Him and a nigga name Red supposed to be hella mixxin on that Mount with that work. I don't know this dude Red, but he supposed to be off the Mount too. He just come home from doing a bid almost a year ago. And if you know Slim like you say you do, then you know he ain't been making no major moves before."

"Nigga you know Red. Dawg use to rock with us before he

went up the road about six years ago. But then again you might not remember him because he use to mix with us when you been in school playing ball. You done seen him before, and ya know what lil bruh? You might be right because them niggas off the Mount is a bunch of slime balls and I heard that nigga Slim been pulling moves on the low."

"Well, that explains the two niggas Trap said kicked in his door and the two niggas that ran up in Tammy house."

"Where they ass at now? Who told you this?"

"Lisa's little cousin, Lil Kris, right before I slapped his ass up with my pistol and robbed his bitch ass. I ain't know where them fuck niggas at, but they ain't on the Mount cause Lil Kris pussy ass been tryna buy work from me."

"Damn bruh, you robbing now?"

"Shit! Niggas robbing us. Why the fuck not?"

"I feel you but you ain't know where Lisa live at?"

"Hell no. But that shit ain't hard to find out."

"Go ahead and see what you can find out. When C-Lo come through, we'll ride through that Mount."

"Bet it up."

***

Chedda, Plat, Lil Rell, and Slam Black were the first people Lil Kris ran into when he got back on the Mount. They were all posted outside of the corner store on the four way.

Chedda looked him up and down and said, "Boy, what happened to your face and why you got blood all over your shirt?"

"Yeah man, what the fuck happen to you zeek?" Plat asked.

"That nigga Slugga robbed me and chopped me with his pistol because I stagged on him. I ain't been tryna give him shit." Lil Kris lied.

"Nigga stop fucking lying. Slugga ain't fucking rob you. That boy and his peoples straight as a fool. Tell somebody else that bullshit." Lil Rell said not believing a word from Lil Kris.

"For real though, Lil Kris. What the hell Slugga got to rob you for? Them niggas major bruh." Plat stated.

"Man, real talk! I flag the nigga down earlier tryna cop some work from zeek. Dawg tell me to ride with him to get it. I was like bet. So, while we riding, he starts asking me all kinds of shit like 'who selling weight round ya?' and I'm like, 'Slim and Red'. Zeek keep asking me questions, so I asked dawg if he the police. But I was just joking with dawg. This nigga started spazzing and whip his pistol out on me and tell me to give him everything. At first, I thought this nigga been bullshitting until he chop me across my face. So, I'm like 'nigga I ain't giving up shit'. But he chop me again over my right eye and cock that shit. So, I just gave him everything because dawg had this crazy look in his eyes. After I gave him everything I had, this muthafucka kick me out his car by the duck pond and I had to walk back here."

By the time Lil Kris had finished telling them what happen to him, everybody was holding their stomachs laughing.

"I see ya'll got jokes. That shit ain't funny zeek!" Lil Kris said getting mad.

"My bad Kris. You right. So, you ain't got no bread?" Chedda asked.

"Yeah, I got a stack duck off and a good bit of pills left, at my gal house. That been my cushion, but now I gotta shoot that to Slim."

"You gonna tell Slim what happened?" Lil Rell asked.

"Hell yeah! What you think?"

"What I think is dawg ain't gonna want to hear that shit. He gonna want his bread." Lil Rell warned him.

"And I'ma pay him what I owe him. I just need one of ya'll to sell me a half of zone so I can make a quick flip."

"I got you my nig." Plat said. "I can't believe Slugga play you like that. How much he get you for?"

"I had twenty-five hundred on me, the twenty-two I owed Slim, and a light three hundred in my pocket. I was gonna pay Slim today, but Lisa said he wasn't around. That's why I was about to cop some work from that jive ass nigga."

"If you had called me the police, I probably would've flip on your ass too." Lil Rell said still laughing.

"You would've asked the same thing if he been asking you a shit load of questions." Chedda said coming to Lil Kris's defense.

"Fuck it. Can't cry over spilt milk. We just got to help you make that bread back. Come on, let's go get this work." Plat stated as they all walked off from the corner store.

***

"Boy I can't wait to see Red bitch ass! All them nigga off the Mount ain't nothing but some slime ball ass niggas! I had a feeling it been somebody we know." C-Lo said from the back seat as he, Tee-Tee, and Slugga headed towards the Mount.

"Since whoever this Red nigga is and Slim want to pull some slime ball shit, we gonna get slime ball too! This for Trap, G-Money, and your unborn seed Cee! Word!" Slugga stated as he turned on a street called Attaway.

"Pull up over there." Tee-Tee pointed. "Let's see if dem boy know where Slim and Red at."

Attaway Towers was some three-story apartments located on Attaway street. When they pulled up at the apartments, they had to ride to the back and come back around because Attaway Towers was a one way in, one way out spot. They wanted to make sure they could get on through if they had to. As they were riding through, about four or five people looked inside the car trying to see who they were.

"Who the fuck is them niggas in that car?" A fella name Black Out asked with his face screwed up.

"Oh, that's Tee Tee. Wussup zeek?" said another fella, named Freddy B. after Tee Tee got out the car.

"Wussup peoples? Ain't none of ya'll know where I can find Slim and Red at?" Tee Tee asked as he got closer to the group of people standing in front of the Towers.

"Nah. Them niggas don't be round ya. We ain't Slim or Red's keeper." Black Out responded with a mug on his face.

"Hold up lil nigga. You ain't even got to come at me like that. I'm just looking for my peeps."

"Everything good my nigga. My dawg just gone off them pills. But what you looking for them boy for?" Freddy B. asked.

"That's our business. You know how the game go. I just need to holla at them boys, so just leave it like that." Tee Tee replied.

"Damn zeek! Shed, I feel if you got business with them boy you would know where they at and how to find them. Plus, they wouldn't have ya'll riding round tryna find them 'specially in the Towers. What's really good Tee Tee? We heard about that bullshit Slugga did to Lil Kris." Freddy B. stated.

"You know what? Fuck it. Everybody get the fuck on the ground and ya bet not run or you won't live to see tomorrow!" Tee Tee demanded pulling out two Glock 45's.

At that moment, C-Lo and Slugga hopped out the car with their guns out to back him up.

"Take everything out ya pockets and kick them muthafuckin shoes off! C-Lo, go pick that shit up and make sure you check they socks!" Tee Tee spat.

"Damn Tee Tee! That's how ya'll rocking now?" Freddy B. asked from the ground.

"Yeah, this how we rocking. Now shut the fuck up!" C-Lo stated as he went to each person picking their money up and checking their pockets, shoes, and socks.

"Wussup now bad ass?" Tee Tee asked talking to Black Out.

Black Out didn't say anything. He was trying to figure out a way to get to the bush he had his gun stashed in without getting shot. He had a feeling Tee Tee was on some bullshit when he got out the car asking for Slim and Red.

Slugga was still standing by the driver door of the car with his Mac 11 pointed at the group of people the ground, hoping that one of them would try to run.

"Tell Slim and Red they ass dead when we find them." C-Lo said as he shot Freddy B. in the ass.

When Slugga, Tee Tee, and C-Lo jumped in the car and rode off, Black Out, along with a couple more people, ran to the bushes where they had their guns stashed at and started shooting at the car.

"Man, drive this car and get us the fuck outta here!" Tee Tee yelled at Slugga as him and C-Lo put their arm out the window and started shooting back.

CHAPTER 14

The next day Trap was propped up in his hospital bed eating his lunch and looking at the news. The anchor lady was reporting an incident that took place the night before near the Attaway Towers.

Just then, Slugga, and C-Lo entered his room.

"Did they say anything about what happen on the Mount last night?" Slugga asked when he saw that Trap was looking at the news.

"That was ya'll?" Trap asked putting two and two together.

Tee-Tee nodded and said, "Remember Red off the Mount who use to rock with us real hard before he went up the road?"

"You already know I remember Red. That's my lil nigga. That been G-Money right hand man. I think he get like 7 or 8 years up the road if I ain't mistaken. Why? Wussup with him?"

"I ran into Lisa, off the Mount, little cousin yesterday and he told me Lisa babydaddy Slim and Red got all the work on the Mount. You and I both know Slim ain't been making no big boy moves before. Plus, Tee Tee said he heard dawg be pulling slime ball moves on the low. And this nigga Red just came home like ten months ago. So, we put two and two together. Two niggas hit you up and two niggas ran up in C-Lo baby mama's mix. I'm willing to bet it was two niggas that fucked G-Money over…and that's your two niggas right there." Slugga stated.

"Damn, I can't see Red mixxin like that. Even though that been G-Money main man, we all was clique tight. All he had to do was holla at us and the nigga would've been straight. G used to always say he couldn't wait until dawg came home. And I never did trust Slim's sneaky ass. I been heard how he been rocking. So, that shit went down on the Mount last night?"

"No, not really. We roll on a couple niggas in the Towers and lay they ass down. I pop one of them in the ass too." C-Lo spoke up.

"I saw that shit on the news. It don't be nothing but a bunch of little niggas that play them Towers. Ya'll should've hit the Bottom of Read or better yet, run up in Lisa spot. She lives on the Mount."

"We rolled on the first group of people we saw. We ain't know exactly where Lisa live at on the Mount. After C-Lo popped Freddy B., the shootout went down, and we had to get the hell on."

Tee Tee replied.

"Let me make a phone call right quick." Trap stated picking up the phone and dialing some numbers. The person on the other end answered. Trap asked a couple questions and then hung up. "She lives in a yellow house in the middle of Blackwell street. It's supposed to be the only yellow house on that street. Don't hurt Lisa if you don't have to. If Slim ain't there, nap that bitch."

***

"How are you doing today Mr. Green?" Dr. Jones, Trap's doctor, asked when he entered Trap's room later that day.

"I guess you can say I'm doing fine mentally, but you the doctor. You know how I'm doing physically. I know one thing; I wish I can hurry up and get the hell up outta here." Trap responded.

"I'm glad to hear that. I got some good news for you. Your wish will be granted tomorrow morning. You're recovering just fine, and we don't need to hold you any longer. Plus, we need this bed." He laughed but soon stopped when he realized that Trap wasn't laughing with him. "I'm just joking about the bed."

"You laughing! You can have this bed. It's about time. I almost thought I was gonna have to move in here."

"I'll have the nurse bring your release papers for you to sign when she comes through doing her rounds tonight so you can have an easy discharge tomorrow. I want you to take your time and don't put too much stress on your body, Mr. Green. You still haven't fully recovered yet. I'll see you in the morning to give you your meds, your prescription forms, and let you know when you'll need to come in for a checkup."

When Dr. Jones left the room, Trap got on the phone and called Tee Tee. He had to call him three times back to back before Tee Tee answered.

"Yo! Wussup? Who this is?" Tee Tee answered sounding agitated.

"This me, Trap. Aye, that thing we talked about earlier, freeze that. They releasing me tomorrow morning. Just peep the scene and see if ya'll see one of them niggas. And make sure ya'll be ya early to pick me up."

"Bet it up. Holla at you tomorrow."

CHAPTER 15

"Boy, what's wrong with your face? Lisa asked when Lil Kris walked through her front door with a bandage over his eye.

"I got robbed leaving your house yesterday. I need to holla at Slim asap. Every time I call his phone he don't answer." Lil Kris replied.

"Who robbed you?" she asked picking up her house phone to dial Slim's number.

"Slugga's bitch ass jam me!"

"Slugga! Slugga robbed you?" she asked surprised. In her mind, she was wondering why Slugga would rob him when he ain't even got it like that.

"Ain't I say tha nigga jam me?" he repeated becoming upset. He didn't like how everybody was acting as if he were lying.

"Don't get mad at me." she said right as Slim answered his

line. "Hey baby, you busy?"

"Nah, I ain't busy. Wussup, everything straight? Where Mann at?" Slim asked answering her question with a question of his own.

"I'm good. Mann at momma house. She gonna keep him for the summer. But listen, Lil Kris right here and he said he need to holla at you."

"I see him calling me. You know I ain't answer for a reason. It must be important if he had you call me."

"Well, I'll let you holla at him." she said passing the phone.

"Wussup Lil Kris? What's so important that you had wifey call me?" Slim asked when Lil Kris got on the phone.

"I got jam up leaving your house yesterday."

"Lil Kris, don't come at me with no bullshit! I done told you I want my money no matter what. I know I shouldn't have fucked with you."

"Nigga, I got your money! I'm about to give it to Lisa! Fuck is you trippin for?"

"My bad, zeek. I thought you were about to hit me with some bullshit. But I out of town right now. I gotta get at you later."

"I wasn't tryna call you with no bullshit. I just wanted to let you know what time it was and give Lisa this bread. Man, you probably won't even believe who jam me."

"Who get you?"

"Slugga fake mix me."

"Who you say?"

"Slugga's bitch ass."

"How he catch you slippin?"

"I had come around here yesterday to holla at you, but you weren't home. So, I just happen to see Slugga riding through and I flagged him down to cop a lil something to hold me down until I got up with you. Zeek told me to ride with him to go get it. Dawg started asking me all kinds of questions and shit. So, I asked the nigga if he tha police. Next thing I know, my face is bleeding and I'm looking down the barrow of a big ass gun."

"What kind of questions zeek been asking you?"

"Shit like who got the work out here. I screamed you and Red's name and zeek really started asking questions."

"What happen after that?"

"That's really all he asked about, because after that he spazzed the fuck out and robbed me. Then I heard that last night, Freddy B. and nem got robbed at the Towers. One of those niggas shot Freddy B. in the ass. Black Out told me that he heard Freddy B.

call one of them Tee-Tee and before they left, they said that you and Red are dead. Shit real outcha family. How you mixxin?"

"I'll hit you when I get back. When you see Plat, Lil Rell, Butta, and Peter Man, tell them boy to call me asap. You and Chedda be careful out there and don't get caught slippin no more. Matter fact, let me holla at Lisa right quick."

"Yeah?" Lisa said getting on the phone.

"I need you to do me a favor."

"Like what?"

"I want you to get something out the cut for Lil Kris."

"Alight Slim, we ain't about to start this shit. You lucky Mann ain't home and Lil Kris my cousin or I ain't been doing this shit."

"Girl, chill with all that wolfing. Why you always got to get jazzy at the mouth in front of people? Everybody know I run shit so ain't no need for you to be fake mixxin."

"Where this shit at before I change my mind? What I am supposed to give him?"

"You still remember how to use the clock like I showed you?"

"Yeah."

***

"Who was that?" Red asked after Slim ended his call. He knew something was wrong by the frustrated look on Slim's face.

"That was Lisa and Lil Kris. We got a problem." Slim answered.

"What kind of problem? Ain't nothing happen to Lisa or Mann init?"

"No, nothing happened to Lisa or Mann. You know we would've been on the road asap. But shit done hit the fan. That nigga Slugga robbed Lil Kris and Tee Tee, C-Lo, and Slugga robbed them lil niggas that be in the Towers. They shot Freddy B., too"

"Who the fuck is Slugga?"

"I know you joking. That's Tee Tee and Trap little brother."

"You talking about little Tony? Last time I saw that lil nigga he been into that football real hard. They call him Slugga now? How you want to mix on this?"

"If you'll let me finish."

"Go head, my bad."

"Let's step outside for a second."

Once outside, Slim told Red everything that Lil Kris had told him over the phone.

"So, what you want to do? You want to get on the road tonight?" Red asked.

"I want to wait until I hear from Plat and the crew. I told Lil Kris that I would holla at him when I got back. I told Lisa I'll be home in a couple of days, plus I got her making moves for me so there's no need to rush. Let's just continue to mix like everything all good until we hear something. We'll leave in a few of days. So, we might as well scream at Cool about that work."

"That's a bet zeek. We might even find us a plug outcha."

"We just might." Slim said as they walked back into the house.

***

Tee Tee was up all-night watching Lisa's house. Lisa had left the house a couple times and he even saw Lil Kris come and go a few times. But there was no sight of Slim or Red. He concluded that they were never gonna show up, but he camped outside of her house anyway.

The next morning, he picked up Slugga and they headed to the hospital to pick up Trap.

Trap was already in the lobby sitting in a wheelchair when he saw Slugga pull up to the hospital. As bad as he wanted to walk out of the hospital, he didn't because he was still in pain, so he allowed the nurse to push him out in the wheelchair. It was hospital procedure. When he got close enough to the car, he got up and used the cane, the hospital gave him, to walk the rest of the way.

"What it do pimp?" Slugga said tapping Tee Tee to wake him up so he could see Trap walking with the cane.

"Nigga fuck you and grab my bags." Trap said to Slugga as he limped to the car feeling happy to finally be able to go home.

Tee Tee grabbed Trap's bags from the nurse and placed them in the trunk. He started to get in the backseat so Trap could sit in the front, but Trap was already seated in the back. Once he was back in the car, Slugga pulled off.

"What's good?" Trap asked as they rode off from the hospital.

"Ain't shit. I camped out in front of ole girl house all night. I ain't see no sign of Slim or Red. Lil bruh, I want you to hear this song I've been listening to all night." Tee Tee replied pulling a CD out his pocket.

"Who is it by?" Trap asked.

"This group called Middle Fingaz. A group Bun B. brought out. The song called is I Got Issues. That shit right." Tee Tee said as he slid the CD into the player and choose the track. Then he turn the volume up and started bobbing his head to the beat. When the second verse came on, he started rapping along.

"I like that mix. Shit, I got issues my damn self. Word!" Trap said when the song went off. "Where C-Lo at?"

"Him and Tammy duck off. Ever since that shit happened at her apartment she's been chilling at his mix." Slugga answered.

"I feel that. Take me by momma house so I can see wussup with her. Aye, Tee Tee, run that song back for me one more time. 8-Ball went all the way off on that shit."

After seeing his mother and promising her that he would come back for dinner later, he told Slugga to take him on the Macon to holla at Meka's mother.

"How you doing Ms. Washington?" Trap greeted her when she opened the door.

"Hey baby, how you doing? I see they finally let you out that hospital. I've been meaning to get up there and see you, but I never could find the time." she replied as they took a seat in the living room. "You want something to drink, baby?"

"No ma'am, I'm straight. I just came by to check on my

mother-in-law and see how you holding up. I wanted to make it to the funeral, but I couldn't leave the hospital."

"I know you did baby, and believe me, Meka knew that you wanted to be there, too. I got some pictures getting developed now. Soon as I pick em up, I'll have some copies made for you. I really appreciate your brothers helping me with the funeral expenses."

"That was really no problem, Ms. Washington. I'm sorry about what happened to Meka. That was supposed to be me in that casket. It's all my fault and I understand if you blame me. Hell, I already blame myself."

"Nonsense, baby. You can't undo God's work. It was Meka's time to go. God called on my baby and now she's up in heaven looking over us. Just be happy he gave you another chance at life. You almost died yourself. No baby, I don't and will not blame you. Nobody can change what is written. Everything in life happens for a reason. Remember that, baby. Now, just because Meka passed on, I don't want that to stop you from coming to see me from time to time, you hear?"

"Yes ma'am."

"Now give me a hug." she smiled. "Travis, you be careful out there. Don't go getting into any trouble. I want to see you again soon."

"Do you need anything?"

"No baby. It ain't nothing you can do to bring her back. Whatever animosity you have with the streets, let God handle it. You'll do that for me right, baby?"

"I'm not about to do nothing stupid. Here's my number. Call me anytime if you need anything."

"Ok, and tell your brothers to come in next time. They don't have to sit in the car like that. They are always welcome in my home." she said standing on the porch waving at them.

***

.Lil Kris was hanging out on the Bottom with Plat, Lil Rell, Peter Man, and Butta. He told them about the conversation he had with Slim the day before.

"He want ya'll to call him," Lil Kris said.

Plat pulled his phone from his hip and went through the numbers until he came to Slim's number. He dialed his line.

"What's up Platinum Stacks?" Slim asked.

"Wussup zeek, what tha mix is family?" Plat responded. "Lil Kris say you wanna holla at us. Everybody right here. Let me put you on speaker phone. "

"Wussup everybody? Here's the mix, me and Red are in a lil

situation with Tee Tee and Slugga and nem. But we ain't tryna bring ya'll in our mix, I just wanted to put everybody on point."

"Slim, you sound crazy. How you mean you ain't tryna bring us in ya'll mix when everything ya'll did is affecting us?" Plat asked.

"I know that shit right." Peter Man agreed.

"Plus, them niggas fuck up when they robbed Lil Kris and shot Freddy B. the other night." Lil Rell voiced.

"Feel what I'm saying! Them niggas ain't had nothing to do with that shit. Fuck putting us on point. It's too late for that. We been on point." Plat stressed.

"It's deeper than just slime balling them niggas. We been hitting them boy on some animosity type shit. A personal beef. Ya feel me?" Slim explained.

"And!? What's that supposed to mean? We outcha big bruh. Fuck them niggas! We all in!" Lil Rell added.

"Ya'll niggas need to get back through and handle up on ya'll business before ya'll business handle up on ya'll." Butta spoke up.

Peter man jumped in and said, "Yeah, my nig, we'll talk about all that shit when ya'll get back. Tell Red I said wussup."

"I right here, family. We got ya'll on speaker phone too." Red responded.

"We should be back between tomorrow or the day after." Slim informed them.

"Hurry up because we been ran out of work over here. We've been hollering at Bone." Plat said.

"He ain't taxing ya'll init?" Slim asked.

"I already told you, us Mount niggas stick together. He keeping it real on the prices." Butta answered.

"Oh yeah, Jig say call him." Lil Kris added.

"A'ight, ya'll let us know if anything else happen out there." Red said before they all hung up.

Later that day, after Slugga and Tee Tee dropped him off, Trap hopped in his car and went to visit his kids. After spending a couple hours with them, he decided to ride around by himself to get his mind right.

He knew he had to get a new place to stay. Although his brothers replaced his furniture with new furniture, had the place thoroughly cleaned and reorganized, it still didn't help him to forget what happened. Trap just didn't feel like it was his home anymore. That place held too many memories.

Trap drove around aimlessly while thinking. He ended up on the Mount, so he decided to ride down Blackwell street. As he crept his car down the narrow road, he saw Lisa standing at her mailbox. He could've easily snatched her up, but instead, he just kept on driving.

He immediately called his brothers to see where they were located, then he asked for directions to G-Money's grave. He let Slugga know that he had a plan and needed them to meet him at G-Money's grave.

Later that night, everyone met up at G-Money's gravesite.

"Why we gotta meet at this grave around all these dead people?" C-Lo asked. He was paranoid being in a graveyard at nighttime.

"Because G-Money is just like family. No fuck that, he is family. So therefore, he's a part of this meeting." Trap stated

Tee Tee had two six packs of Icehouse that he had picked up from the store on the way there. He opened two bottles and poured them on G-Money's grave. Then he passed everybody a bottle. They all drank in silence, caught up in their own thoughts.

After the first six pack was gone Slugga rolled up five cigars full of loud. He sparked two of the blunts and put them into rotation, then Trap started breaking down his plans for the next day. After everybody agreed with the plan, they sat back reminiscing about the good times when G-Money was alive.

Before they left, Tee Tee poured the last two bottles of Icehouse on G-Money's grave and said, "Sleep in peace homie."

Then they all got into their cars and went their separate ways.

CHAPTER 16

Cool Hand, Red, and Slim were in Cool Hand's back yard sitting in some lounge chairs by the built-in pool, sipping syrup and rotating a blunt while they talked amongst themselves. Tiny, Boo, Key Key, Lee Lee, Tiffany, and Carla were all having a good time in the pool enjoying the nice sunny day.

"We plan on slabbing out tomorrow or the day after. But we need a favor from you." Red said.

"It all depends on what the favor is." Cool Hand replied.

"We're tryna get some work for the low low."

"Mane, you know Cool don't mix up with no dope. But Key Key got a cousin out in Texas who's a heavy hitter in the weight game. I can get her to call him, and if everything is a go, we can ride there tomorrow."

"Well, tell her to mix that mix like ASAP."

"Hey Key Key, look her baby." Cool Hand called out.

Key Key stepped out the pool in a two-piece Baby Phat bikini set. All Slim and Red could say was damn as she walked toward them with water running down her body and her pussy lips poking out the fabric of her bikini.

"What's up baby?" she asked as she stood before Cool Hand.

"Red and Slim want to meet your cousin out in Texas. So, call him and see what's poppin. If he's good with it, tell him we'll be down that way first thing tomorrow."

Key Key left to make the phone call. Ten minutes later, she came back to ask Red and Slim what they were trying to spend.

"50, probably 60." Red responded.

She left again then came back to let them know that she got them a deal for 65."

"What kind of deal?" Red asked.

"He gonna give y'all five of them things since I told him y'all my people. He charges fifteen a piece, so y'all getting the fifth one for five." she said breaking everything down. But the deal was really five for the 60. She was charging the extra five to get her cut.

"Hell yeah! We'll take that deal!" Slim stated.

***

Trap was at CVS picking up his medication and a ten pack of 100cc syringe needles. As he was leaving the drug store, he called Tee Tee to make sure everybody was on South Rhett. Then he rode over there.

Once he got there, they all piled up in a Caravan with light tinted windows that Slugga rented from a smoker he knew. Once they got on Blackwell street, they parked two houses down from Lisa's house and waited on the mailman to come. Thirty minutes of waiting, the mailman finally arrived and placed the mail into Lisa's mailbox. Not long after, Lisa came outside to get her mail. She saw the van on the side of the road a couple of houses down from hers but thought nothing of it and continued to her mailbox.

While she was standing at the mailbox looking through her mail the van rolled up behind her. She heard the slide door open and when she turned around, Trap had his .357 pointed at her.

"Bitch, you bet not run or scream." he said through clench teeth.

Lisa was too scared to move or scream. She just stood there looking at them in shock.

"Don't look surprised, bitch." C-Lo said as he climbed out of the car. He grabbed her and put her in the seat between him and Tee Tee.

Trap took the mail, that she was still holding, out of her hand. Then he got out of the van and limped to Lisa's front door, that was still open. He dropped the mail on a table then he used his shirt to grab the doorknob and close the door. Once he was back in the van they rode off as if nothing happen. After returning to South Rhett, they took Lisa inside and Tee Tee tied her to one of the kitchen chairs.

"Trap, why are you doing this?" Lisa cried.

"Oh, you ain't know? Let me show you." he said pulling up his shirt so she could see where he was shot. Then he pulled down his pants and underwear so she could also see the burnt skin on the head of his penis. "This is what your baby daddy and his partna Red did to me before they killed Meka."

"And you had the nerve to show up to Meka's funeral bitch?!" Slugga asked after he spit in her face.

"I don't believe you!" she screamed using her shoulder to wipe the spit off her face. "Trap, you know how me and Meka rock. That's my girl. You honestly think I would be a part of what happened to her?"

"I ain't never said you did." Trap replied.

"So, why y'all ya'll kidnap me? I don't even believe Slim or Red had anything to do with what happened to you. But if they did, what I got to do with it?"

"Bitch, I ain't tryna hear all that bullshit! Meka ain't had shit to do with it neither. It is what it is. Now where your punk ass baby daddy at?" Trap asked while fixing his clothes.

"I haven't seen him in about four days. Trap, we all go too far back for this. What are y'all about to do with me?" she cried.

"To be honest, my intentions were to kill you just like they killed Meka, G-Money, and C-Lo's unborn seed, but since me and you go way back as you put it, I came up with another conclusion." He stepped closer to her and said, "This is what I'm gonna do for you, Lisa. I'm gonna give you a shot of this." he pulled a bundle of heroin out of his pocket and held it up to her face. Then he asked Slugga to grab a spoon out of the kitchen. "Aye C-Lo, go get them needles out of the glove compartment in the car."

Lisa's eyes widen when she realized what Trap was planning to do. She started squirming in the chair trying to get loose. After struggling to no avail, she started screaming and calling for help.

"Bitch, shut the fuck up with all of that damn screaming!" Trap said and backhand slapped her across the face. Which only made her cry and scream louder. "Tee Tee, find me something to gag this bitch mouth and let me hold your belt."

After Silencing Lisa, Trap wrapped the belt around her left arm and told C-Lo to hold her arm down on the table. She panicked even more as she watched Trap place a spoon, pack of needles, a glass of water, a pack of Newport cigarettes, and a bundle of dope out on the table.

Trap took a bag from the bundle of dope and dumped the brown powder onto the spoon. He then stuck his finger into the glass of water and let three drops of water drip onto the spoon. Next, he grabbed a cigarette, removed its filter and put it on the spoon to suck up the dope. After that, he took a needle from the pack and stuck the needle into the filter. Once the drew up the amount that he needed, he cleared out the air bubbles and turned his attention to Lisa.

"I hope you're paying attention because this is about to be your permanent high." Trap said stuck the needle in her arm and release its contents.

Lisa's eyes grew really big and almost instantly she started hearing a humming noise in her head. The room started spinning and to her, it seemed like everything was moving in slow motion. Trap was talking to her, but she couldn't understand him. Five minutes later, her body became limp and her head dropped down to her chest. Trap removed the gag from her mouth and drool rolled down her chin.

She came out of her nod ten minutes later and started throwing up.

"One of y'all get me something to clean this up." Trap

instructed as he untied Lisa.

C-Lo brought him a towel and he began cleaning her face. When he went to remove her shirt, he noticed that she wasn't wearing a bra. Her titties were nice. The way they sat up, all perfect, firm, and round, made Trap's dick hard. He licked his lips and wondered what the rest of her looked like.

"Ain't no rubbers in ya?" Trap asked Slugga and C-Lo.

"Look in the draw next to the bed. And I got next." Slugga stated.

"All of us about to fuck this bitch. Ain't no fun if my niggas can't get none." Trap said as he pulled Lisa up from the chair and took her to the bedroom.

They all took turns having sex with her. Every hour, Trap shot Lisa up with dope. After the sixth time, he knew he had her hooked. He told everybody they could ride out and stayed behind to keep an eye on her. He left her in the room and went out to the living room to order food and watch TV. Eventually, he dozed off.

Lisa woke up in the middle of the night unaware of where she was. Her body was aching and the room was dark. When she moved to get up, she felt a wave of nausea hit her and started throwing up. Trap opened the door to find Lisa laying on the floor naked in her own vomit. She was shaking like she had a case of bad chills.

"Pl-please help m-m-me." she stuttered as she held her stomach while lying in the fetal position.

Trap went back to the kitchen to grab the dope and utensils so he could shoot her up with another dose. He had to smile to himself because he knew his plan was working. Seeing her shaking on the floor like that, let him know that her body was craving the dope. Before he gave her another shot, he cleaned her up.

Once she was doped up, he had sex with her again. He couldn't get enough of Lisa's pussy. He used to try to fuck her back in the day, but she would never give him the time of day.

When he was done, he left a bag of dope on the table next to the bed along with everything she would need so she could shoot herself up. Then he went back out to the living room.

Tee Tee and Slugga returned to the spot around 10 AM the following morning to find Trap resting on the couch with a smile on his face.

"Nigga, wake your ass up! In ya smiling in your sleep and

shit." Slugga said kicking his foot.

Trap jumped up and grabbed his pistol from under the pillow. "What the fuck is wrong with y'all scaring me like that?" he said after he realized it was his brothers waking him up.

"Nigga, you're the one in ya slipping." Tee Tee said tossing him a Burger King bag.

"Where ole girl at? She still in the room?" Slugga asked.

"Yeah, she still in there. Soon as I'm done eating, we can drop her back off to her house." Trap answered.

"I'm about to get me some more of that pussy while you eat." Slugga said walking towards the room.

"Let me know if she use that bag of dope I left in there with her." Trap yelled behind him.

When Slugga walked into the room, Lisa was laying on the bed high out her mind.

"Yeah, she done mix that mix." Slugga answered peeking his head out the door.

Thirty minutes later, they dropped Lisa back off to her house. Lisa was so high that she didn't know if she was coming or going.

Tee Tee helped Trap walk her to her door just in case someone was in the house. When Trap turned the doorknob, the door was still unlocked so he knew nobody was in there. They took her to the living room and sat her down on the couch.

Trap reached into his pocket, pulled out six bags of dope and placed them on the table in front of her, along with two needles and the half empty pack of Newport. He also wrote his number on a piece of paper and put it in Lisa's pocket. He told her to call him anytime. Lisa was so out of it she didn't even hear him.

As they left, Trap used his shirt to wipe his fingerprints off of everything he touched. He and Tee Tee got in the car and Slugga pulled off.

***

At the time that Trap was dropping Lisa off at her house, Slim, Red, Cool Hand, Key Key, Boo, and Tiny were on their way to Texas. A few hours later, they were pulling up to a ranch style house on the out skirts of Houston in an area called Alvin.

They were greeted by a guy wearing a cowboy hat, cowboy boots, tight denim jeans, and button up flannel shirt with a leather vest over it.

"Who the fuck is that?" Red asked.

"That's Key Key's cousin. The one y'all came to meet." Cool Hand answered. "Oh, don't get it confused. The cover of that book don't match the story inside. The boy got it, ye-ain-know?"

"Looks sure can be deceiving." Slim stated.

"You ain't never lied." Boo echoed.

"How y'all doing? Did y'all have a safe trip?" Beatle, Key Key's cousin, asked from his porch. His southern drawl was thick.

"Yeah, we had a safe trip, Cousin Beatle." Key Key answered as she gave him a hug.

"Alrighty. Who you got wit ya?"

"This me and Cool's friends from Charleston, South Carolina. This is Red, that's Slim, Tiny, and Boo." she said pointing to everyone as she called their name.

"I see we got us some Geechee boys." he said as he shook everybody's hand. "Y'all folks know how to ride a horse?"

"Charleston is the city, zeek. Ain't nobody riding no horse unless it's at a parade or by them police from downtown." Red replied.

"No disrespect, but we ain't come here to ride no horses." Slim stated.

"Slow down, rabbit. Just take ya time my man. Give Key Key

the keys to the car and y'all take a ride with me on my horses. Please don't insult my hospitality." Beatle said.

Red gave Key Key the car keys and they followed Beatle to his horse stable. For a hour or better, they rode the horses around Beatle's ranch talking about everything except what they came there for.

While they were riding around, Beatle's cell phone started ringing. He answered it and said a few words before hanging up. Then they headed back to the horse stable, where Key Key was awaiting them.

"Well fellas, everything is taken care of. Y'all can go ahead and get on y'all way." Beatle said.

"Hold up, bruh! How you mean everything taken care of? We ain't talk about nothing the whole time we been on them damn horses zeek!" Slim stated.

"I done handled everything." Key Key spoke up.

"So, where the stuff at?" Red asked wanting to see the product.

"It's packed in the door panel and I already got the money out the bag y'all had in the car." Key Key answered.

"It was more than 65 stacks in that bag!" Slim said heading towards the car.

"I only took sixty-five out. Everything is good. Trust me, Slim. I wouldn't play with ya'll's money. Cool, holla at ya boy." Key Key stated.

"Mane, Red, tell ya man to give my girl some kind of credit. Everything good baby. Y'all can check everything out when we get back to my pad." Cool Hand stated.

"Aye Slim, calm down zeek. You got to realize we ain't coping work out the back yard of a local nigga. We dealing with a major nigga. Plus, if he play the game fuck up, we'll just roll back on his ass. Feel me?" Red whispered to Slim.

"You right my nigga. I'm still gonna count our bread before we slide, bruh." Slim replied. "My bad Key Key and Cool." he apologized.

"If y'all ever need to get back at me, just get at me through Key Key." Beatle stated.

"That's wussup." Red said as they walked towards their car.

"Y'all be careful on that road, ya hear? Maybe next time y'all decide to come through, I'll take y'all to a couple of clubs in Wichita Falls and show y'all how us country boys get down. Don't let the clothes fool ya, we know how to party out here."

"That's a bet." Red and Slim said in unison.

Key Key, Boo, and Tiny rode back to Tennessee together in

the car that had the drugs in it while Red, Slim, and Cool Hand followed behind them in Cool Hand's SUV.

"Dig it, Slim. I know that transaction was strange but you got to understand that Beatle is at a level where he don't touch dope no more. I ain't in the dope game, but I know its levels to that shit. Beatle is a straight up cat. He good peoples." Cool Hand stated.

"I feel ya Cool, I feel ya."

It wasn't as late when they returned back to Cool Hand's house, but it was too late to get back on the road. So, Red and Slim decided to wait until morning to get on the head home. Tiny and Boo wanted to do some last-minute shopping, so they left to go to the mall with Key Key.

Slim and Red went outside to open the door panel on the car and took one of the bricks out. They wanted to make sure that everything was all good. Afterwards, they headed out to the Crest to get some more syrup from Cool Hand's people.

On the way there, Cool Hand called John John to let him know that he was on the way. John John already outside waiting on them when they arrived. Slim and Red bought three pints and Cool Hand bought one.

"Wussup with Gotti? He still on the road?" Cool Hand asked.

"I guess so. I ain't seen him yet." John John replied.

"I dig it. Hold it down playa."

"A'ight, Cool. Be easy."

Back at Cool Hand's house, they sat out back sipping their syrup and talking with a blunt in rotation.

"When y'all playa's coming back?" Cool Hand asked.

"Ain't no telling. I guess when we got some free time." Red answered.

"I know one thing, next time we come through, we ain't bringing our gals with us." Slim stated.

"Shit, zeek. You need to come to the Chuck and fuck with us." Red stated.

"Mane, you already know what happened the last time I came to South Carolina. With all that mixing up y'all doing down there, ain't no telling what will happen. But who knows, the wind might blow me that way." Cool Hand said.

"Do that because we want to show you the same love you showed us. Real talk." Red stated.

"Ye-ain-know!" Slim said and everybody started laughing.

***

The next morning, Slim, Red, Tiny and Boo got on the road to head home. It was 9:30 p.m. when they arrived back in Charleston. They would've gotten there sooner , but they had to be careful on the road since they were riding dirty.

They pulled up in Tiny's mother backyard because her mother had a shed behind her house. Red called Cool Hand to let him know they had made it back safe, while Slim took the panels off the car doors. In one door, he pulled out three bricks and in the other door, he pulled out two bricks and a half. There was a note taped to the half brick.

Red read the note out loud. "Just a little token of my southern hospitality, Big Tex."

"I like that country ass nigga! We most definitely gotta holla back at dawg." Slim said.

"I'ma hit Cool up tomorrow and tell him to tell Key Key we said nice looking out. And to have her tell her cousin we got that note and we most definitely gonna be fucking with him." Red said.

Tiny and Red decided to leave baby K with Tiny's mom for another night so they could hang out with Boo and Slim. After they made it to Red's place, they ordered food from Dave's restaurant. Slim stepped away to call and check on Lisa, it she didn't answer. He figured she was probably asleep and left a message letting her know that he would be home the next day.

CHAPTER 17

The following day, Lisa was walking around the house nervous. She really didn't know what she was nervous about. She checked her voicemail on her cell phone and heard Slim's message, so she knew he would be home soon.

She sat in the bed and tried to read a book, but she couldn't focus on it because she was too busy wondering if Slim would be able tell whether she had been using. She knew she would have to tell him what happened, but she didn't know how. So, she decided that she would just wait to see if he noticed it first.

Slim came home and went up to the bedroom where he found Lisa.

"Where Mann at?"

"He's over at momma's house. He been over there since you left." she answered while avoiding eye contact.

"I brought y'all a few things back." he said holding up the bags in his hands. "I got some more shit in the front room."

All Lisa could say was, "Thanks."

Her lack of enthusiasm alarmed Slim.

"Damn baby, wussup with you? You got something on your mind?"

At that moment, she started crying.

"Girl, what the fuck is wrong with you!?"

"Why are you yelling at me?" she whined.

"My bad, but why the hell are you crying? I just asked if something was on your mind; I didn't expect you to get upset."

"Trap and his brothers kidnap me the other day." she blurted out.

Slim paused for a second. He had to make sure that he'd heard her right. "They did what? I'm gonna kill those muthafuckas!"

Sniffling, Lisa added, "They got me hooked on heroin then raped me." she opened the drawer on the nightstand and pulled out the dope. "I'm a junkie!" she cried.

"Oh, hell naw!" he screamed punching a hole into the wall. "Where did they take you?" he asked with fire in his eyes and venom in his voice.

"I don't know, Slim. I can't remember." she cried. She never saw Slim that angry and seeing him like that made her cry even harder.

At that moment, Slim went to the bed to comfort her.

"I'm gonna help you get through this, okay baby girl? I swear I got you." he whispered in her ear as he held her.

Lisa shook her head up and down then asked, "Slim, did you kill Meka?"

"Do you really want me to answer that?"

"No baby, just hold me. Please don't leave me tonight. I'm scared."

"Baby, I ain't going nowhere and you ain't gotta be scared because I'm right here for you."

"Slim, when you catch Trap, can I kill him?"

"Don't worry about that right now, a'ight? Let's just lay here together."

Later that day while Lisa was resting, Slim called Red to tell him about what happened to Lisa while they were in Tennessee.

"I'm on my way down there right now zeek." Red said through the phone.

"Just fall back. I'll get up with you tomorrow." Slim stated.

"Hell naw, man! Them niggas know where you lay your head at zeek! I told you that you need to move from off that Mount! Either y'all coming downtown or we're coming to the north. Plus, sis gonna give you hell when she can't get no dope in her system. Trust me, I know."

"I feel you. Let me get some things together and me and Lisa will be down there. A'ight?"

"Type-of-thing! I'll see y'all when y'all get down ya."

Once Slim and Lisa made it down to Red's place, Tiny took her upstairs to Kaela's room so she could rest. Afterwards, she went to her room to call Boo and tell her what happened.

Slim and Red were downstairs in the living room talking.

"They got my gal hooked on that shit, bruh!" Slim said to Red as if it was his first time saying it.

"Big bruh, I know that shit fucking with you but we gotta get Lisa right first before we get at them niggas. I feel like this shit is my fault too, so you know I'm all in with you. But on the real though, we about to catch hell with sis for the next few days." Red replied.

"You know Lisa asked me to let her mix Trap. And real talk, I'm thinking about letting her do it."

"It is what it is. If it had been Tiny, I would've let her do it but that's your call. Just know I'm with you to the end."

"That's wussup. We need to call everybody and let them know we're back."

"No zeek. You need to call your people. I been call my peeps."

After Slim called everybody, he and Red sat in the kitchen breaking a couple of bricks own into quarter pieces so they could get everybody right for the next day.

"Damn, let me hit Jig up. I was supposed call that nigga a while ago." Slim said as he began dialing Jig's number.

"Wha tha mix is family?" Jig answered.

"You tell me zeek. How you rocking?"

"Man zeek, I been tryna get at you. I need some of them grippas you got. You still straight init?"

"Yeah everything mix, but I ain't making no moves tonight."

"Well, you should've waited until tomorrow to call me. But fuck it, I done waited this long another day won't kill me. Just make sure you get at me asap. Oh, and do you have some of that white, too?"

"Yeah, but why you ain't holla at your cousin Bone?"

"Damn dawg, you act like you ain't tryna get this paper. What kind of question is that?"

"No, it ain't like that. I was just saying."

"Family tore up right now, but I can spend my money with who I want to spend it with. So, you got some white or not?"

"Yeah, I got it."

"Bet. I'll holla at you in the morning."

"A'ight."

"Oh yeah, I almost forgot. Sheezy said he need to holla at you and Red."

"What's dawg number?"

Jig read the number off to Slim.

"Bet it up. I'll holla at you tomorrow."

"Mix."

Slim ended the call.

"Me and you can split that sell." Slim said to Red.

"Bet. What did he want?"

"A half and 400 pills."

"Jig doing the damn thing behind North Charleston High school. Why he ain't holla at Bone for the white?"

"He said Bone was tore up. But yeah, Jig quacking behind that school. He thinks he's slick though. The only reason he buying a half is because it's from us. If he were buying from Bone, he would've buy a brick or better. It's all good. I need to hit up Sheezy and see what the fuck he wants."

"Who the fuck is this?" Sheezy answered.

"Damn my nigga. That's how you answer your pipe?" Slim asked.

"This my shit. I can answer it any way I want to. Now, who the fuck is this?"

"This Slim my nigga. Wussup wit cha?"

"Oh. What's good my nigga? I been about to hang up on your ass." Sheezy laughed.

"Shit. Just tryna pay the bills, feel me? Jig said you wanted to holla at me and Red."

"Yeah my nigga. How about I ran into Tee Tee and Slugga the other day. They been asking about you and Red. Y'all know them boy got change on y'all head?"

"For real? How much?"

"They say fifteen a piece."

"That's it? You're right, that is change. I thought we would've been worth more than that. Where you see them clowns at?"

"By Captain D's on Rivers avenue. Dem boy be on South Rhett somewhere."

"That's wussup. Call me tomorrow. I got a lil' deal for you. And I got something extra for you for the heads up."

"That's a bet." Sheezy said.

Slim hung up and turned to Red. "Bruh, let me trip you out. Sheezy say Tee Tee and Slugga got a price on our heads."

"How much we worth?" Red asked.

"A punk ass fifteen stacks a piece."

"Damn, that's it? We done fuck them niggas pockets up." Red said laughing.

"That shit sound funny, but on the real though it's some hungry ass niggas out there who'll bust our heads for less than that. Real talk."

Before Red could respond to Slim's statement, Lisa started screaming from upstairs. They both ran upstairs to check on her. When they got to the top floor, Tiny was standing in the doorway debating on whether she should go in or stay put.

Lisa was on the bed shaking and sweating. She rocked back and forth while holding her stomach.

"It hurts." she moaned in pain. Then she started throwing up.

Slim pushed pass Tiny to get into the room. As he held her in his arms, he told Tiny to get some towels.

"Please give me a hit so the pain will stop." Lisa begged.

Red had warned that Lisa's detox wasn't going to be easy. He knew because his mother was an ex-heroin addict. He recalled the times when he had to watch her go through withdrawal.

Tiny went to get a couple of towels like she was instructed. When she returned, she began cleaning Lisa's vomit up from the floor.

For the remainder of the night, Lisa ran Slim, Red, and Tiny crazy. She went from crying, to aching, to screaming that she wanted to die, to begging for some dope. Nobody got any sleep that night.

***

The next morning went the same way. Tiny told Red and Slim to go ahead and handle their business and that she would stay and watch over Lisa for a few hours. Even though Slim didn't want to leave her, Red tried ensure him that everything would be ok. Slim wasn't convinced, but he left anyway. The plan was to meet everybody on the Bottom at Junky Randy house. When they got to Randy's house Plat, Butta, Peter Man, Lil Rell, Chedda, Lil Kris, Lil V, D. Money, Booja, and Sheezy were there waiting. After collecting money from the ones that owed them, Slim and Red hit everybody off with some product. Once everyone was taken care of, Slim pulled Sheezy to the side. Red handed Sheezy five stacks and some extra product.

"Call us if you see any of them niggas and you'll get more of this with another five stacks. Nice looking on the heads up, bruh." Slim stated.

"To be honest, that info was for free. Y'all ain't had to give me shit, but I damn sure will take it." Sheezy said with a smile on his face. "I'll never give my dawgs up. Them niggas crazy. It's Mount for life. I had Tee Tee number written down, but I couldn't find it this morning. If I find it, I'll hit you on the pipe asap."

"Say less. We'll get up with y'all boy later. Y'all niggas be careful. Aye, Lil Kris. Look here for a min." Slim said as they walked outside.

"Wussup bruh?" Lil Kris asked.

"Don't repeat what I'm about to say."

"Ok."

"Listen, Trap and them bitch ass niggas snatched Lisa and shot her up with dope. Now she's hooked."

"Where she at? She okay?" Lil Kris asked.

"She good, but she ain't on B. Dub."

"Man, I outcha! Call me if you need me. I swear to God if I see one of them niggas, I'm blasting on sight! Good word!" Lil Kris said as he walked off. "Tell my cousin I love her and I got her."

After Slim and Red left the Bottom, they went to Jig's spot. Jig wasn't pressed for conversation. He was mad because he had to wait all morning for Slim and Red to roll on him. It was almost three in the afternoon when they finally made it to him. So, they made the drop and went back to Red's house. Slim was anxious to get back to Lisa and Red had Dolla and Crunch waiting on him.

Once inside the house, Slim turned his phone off. He didn't want anybody to bother him while he catered to Lisa for the next five days.

***

On the fifth day, Lisa was doing better. She had lost a little bit of weight due to her not eating, but her appetite picked back up and she was eating again. Seeing her regaining her strength, made Slim feel a little more at ease. When he got a moment to himself, he turned his phone back on to check his messages and noticed that his voicemail was full. He was only interested in two messages, and they were from Sheezy and Boo. They both had called his line numerous times. He returned Sheezy's call first.

"Wussup Slim? It's about time you return a nigga call. I almost thought you ain't had want them niggas." Sheezy joked.

"Naw, it ain't been like that. I just been out the mix for a few days. What's the word?"

"I found dawg number. What you want me to do?"

"Call that nigga and tell him you saw me earlier. Then ask him what he want you to do when you see me again."

"Say no more. I got ya family."

After Slim hung up with Sheezy, he called Boo. They talked on the phone for about thirty minutes before Sheezy called back. Slim told Boo he would call her back later. Then he switched over to Sheezy.

"Yo." Slim answered.

"Dawg say he want me to call him back asap when I see y'all and he been real amp up."

"Where are you gonna be in an hour?"

"I don't know, but I'm outcha though. Just hit me and I'll meet you between Filbin Creek apartments and 1251."

"A'ight. I'll hit you in a lil while once I put some shit together." Slim ended the call and went back to Lisa.

CHAPTER 18

Two hours later, Slim, Red, Peter Man, Butta, and Sheezy met up at the apartment in 1251.

Slim turned to Sheezy and said, "Call that nigga and tell him you just saw me and Red go into an apartment around ya. Tell him to hurry up because you don't know how long we'll there."

Sheezy dialed Tee Tee's number.

"Yo, who this?" Tee Tee answered.

"This Sheezy, my nig. Where you at?"

"Why? Wussup?"

"Red and Slim."

"Where?"

"They over ya in 1251. They just got here about five minutes ago. I don't know how long they gonna here, so hurry up and don't forget my check. I'll be sitting on the steps in the first breeze way."

"Make sure you call me if them leave." Tee Tee said then hung up.

***

"Who that been?" C-Lo asked from the passenger seat.

"Sheezy. He said Red and Slim are in 1251. Call Trap and Slugga and tell them we about to come snatch them."

"Fuck that. We can handle that shit ourselves. Ain't no telling how long they about to be over there, plus we ain't far. Let's ride on them niggas." C-Lo said checking his gun to make sure he had one in the chamber.

***

Red and Slim were posted in a downstairs apartment peeking through the window blinds waiting for Tee Tee to show up. Peter Man and Butta were duck off in a van that was parked in the lot outside of the apartment building. Sheezy was sitting on the steps smoking a cigarette like he told Tee Tee he would be.

When Tee Tee pulled up to the apartment complex, he parked right in front of the apartment where Sheezy was sitting. As he got

236

out the car, he told C-Lo to hang back while he talked with Sheezy.

C-Lo remained in the car as instructed. He was too busy focusing on Tee Tee that he never noticed Butta and Peter Man creeping up on both sides of the car until it was too late. He tried to go for his pistol, but Butta and Peter Man were already shooting at the car.

Boom, boom, boom, pop, pop, pop!

Butta and Peter Man continued to put slugs in C-Lo's body and the car. The moment Tee Tee heard the shots behind him, he knew it was a set up. He instantly pulled out both of his Glock 45's. He shot Sheezy two times. One bullet hit him in the arm and the other hit him in the chest. He let off one more round, but didn't stick around long enough to see where it him. Tee Tee took cover and began returning fire back at Peter Man and Butta.

Butta dove behind a parked car just in time to avoid getting shot, but Peter Man wasn't so lucky. He caught a bullet in the neck and chest. He laid about five feet away from Butta drowning in his own blood.

Once Tee Tee saw that Peter Man had gone down, he focused his aim at the car that Butta was hiding behind unaware that they weren't alone. As he was shooting at Butta, someone began shooting at him. Before he could react, a bullet hit him in the shoulder causing him to drop one of his guns. Tee Tee dropped to the ground and looked back thinking that it was Sheezy who had shot him, but to his surprise the shooter turned out to be Red and Slim. They were coming at him fast. Tee Tee pushed through the pain just in time to grab his gun and fire back at them.

When Red and Slim saw Tee Tee hit the ground, they thought they had killed him. They moved in to finish him off and were met with bullets. Tee Tee had come back up shooting at them. As they ran for cover, Tee Tee took off running while continuing to shoot in their direction. One of his guns ran out of bullets. He knew he was outnumbered and didn't want to use up the bullets he had left shooting in the blind in case he got trapped off again. It was about survival and the only thing on his mind was getting away.

Seeing that Tee Tee wasn't shooting anymore Red and Slim figured he was out of bullets. They came out of their duck off spot and started shooting at him again. Tee Tee was running zig zag so they couldn't get a clear shot as he got away.

After the shooting had stopped, people came out of their homes to see what was going on. Butta walked over to where Peter

Man laid dead and closed his eyes. Sheezy was also dead. The last bullet that Tee Tee shot at him entered his forehead and blew out the back of his head.

Tee Tee didn't stop running until he made it to Remount road. It was a blessing when he saw the city bus coming down the street. Just as he hopped on the bus and rode off, he heard sirens wailing in the distance.

"Damn, that was a close one." he said to himself as grabbed a seat at the back of the bus. He had forgotten about his injured arm until his adrenaline wore off. That's when he felt the pain. It was a good thing that the bus wasn't crowded because he didn't have to worry about people looking at him.

"That lil nigga try to double cross me. Damn! Them bitch ass niggas kill C-Lo. I hope I killed Sheezy bitch ass." he said continuing to talk to himself.

***

Back at 1251, Slim, Red, and Butta were hopping in the van they had arrived in. There was nothing they could do for Peter Man or Sheezy. So, they searched both men's pockets and removed any drugs, money, or weapons they had. Butta grabbed Peter Man's gun and they all left before the police arrived.

Instead of dropping Butta back off on the Mount, they all headed downtown to Red's spot. Once they got there, they didn't have to worry about Lisa or Tiny because Tiny was doing Lisa hair upstairs. Red grabbed three Styrofoam cups and made everybody a drink. Slim rolled up a few boonk blunts and passed everybody a pill. They sipped and got high while talking about what took place earlier.

***

Tee Tee got off the bus by Captain D's on Rivers avenue and took a short walk to some apartments on South Rhett. When he came through the door, Slugga and Trap were passing a blunt back and forth while playing a basketball game on the PlayStation 4.

"Damn nigga, what the fuck happen to you?" Slugga asked when he noticed Tee Tee.

"What the fuck! Where C-Lo at? Ain't y'all been together?" Trap asked pushing pause on the game and getting up from his chair.

"Bruh, that shit just went down on the Mount! Slugga, remember that lil nigga Sheezy we had seen by Captain D's a few days back?" Tee Tee asked.

"Yeah, I remember." Slugga answered.

"That nigga double crossed me and C-Lo. C-Lo got hit up in the mix. I barely made it off the Mount with my life."

"You left C-Lo?" Trap asked.

"Bruh, that nigga dead! They put so many slugs in him and my car, it's impossible for him or anybody to live through that shit. I had to dip on feet and catch the bus here."

"You a'ight?" Trap asked.

"In and out. Hurt like a muthafucka but I'm good."

"Man, you sure C-Lo dead?" Slugga asked.

"Ain't no way family could've taken that many slugs and live. I did shoot Sheezy's bitch ass like two or three times. It was so quick. I don't know if I did any damage, but I know for sure I kill one of them niggas. I hope Sheezy ass dead, too. Bruh, it been so much shooting out there. I'm talking about I'm shooting one way, then Red and Slim come out of nowhere then I'm shooting at them. Them pussy muthafuckas ain't know that I'ma gun slanga and they fucking with a real live soldier." he said holding up his two Glocks.

"You need to clean your arm before that shit get infected." Trap stated.

"I know. We riding for C-Lo tonight?" Slugga asked.

"Lil bruh, you already know what time it is." Trap replied.

***

Detective Cummbee and Detective Deckard arrived at the scene of the shooting and began scanning the area.

"Looks like we just walked into a war zone with all of these shell casings on the ground." Detective Deckard stated.

"You can say that again. You know that's Carlos Smalls in that car." Detective Cummbee replied.

"They sure as hell filled him up with bullets. You think this has anything to do with Travis Green?"

"I'd put my badge on it. Carlos Green didn't stand a chance. The gun that was found on him wasn't even fired. I told you from the beginning that family was something to keep an eye on, but you didn't want to believe me."

"What we do we do now? We can't go locking people up on a few hunches. As you already know, these people aren't about to talk."

"You got a point, but we can start with fingerprints and finding out who this car is registered to. Then we start issuing warrants. Hopefully, no more dead bodies will pop up before we solve this case. The only thing I'm confused about is who they're beefing with."

"Maybe we'll find something out once we identify the other two John Does."

"I hope so... I hope so."

***

Later that night, Trap was behind the wheel of a stolen Lebaron with the top down heading towards the Mount. Tee Tee was in the passenger seat clutching a Mac-11 and Slugga was in the back seat nursing an AK-47 with two 30 round clips taped together.

It was a little crowd at the bottom of Read street. Plat, Lil Rell, Lil V., D. Money, Chedda, and a few more people were out there. Everybody was caught up talking about what they heard took place earlier that day in 1251. Nobody was paying attention to the car creeping down the street with no lights on, until Plat happened to look up the street.

"Oh shit! Get the fuck down!" Plat scream as he dove on Lil Rell. Slugga let the choppa rip one way while Tee Tee let his Mac spit the other way. Due to the fact that the Bottom was a one way street, Trap had to turn the car around in order to get off the street. As he was riding out, Plat and a few other people started shooting back. The last thing they saw were the taillights of the Lebaron turning right onto Remount road. Everybody got up from the ground except D. Money and another little fella, who was still on the ground screaming. Lil Kris was on the other side of the street holding his arm. He caught a bullet as he was coming through the cut. People were also in their apartments screaming. Chedda ran over to where D. Money laid, while Lil V. checked on the other fella.

"Call an ambulance!" Chedda screamed out.

At that moment, everybody heard more shooting from a distance. The noise came from the direction of Blackwell street. After leaving the Bottom, Trap and his crew drove over to B. Dub street and pulled up in front of Slim's house. Trap took the choppa from Slugga and started emptying the clip on Slim's place. Then they took off.

"That's for C-Lo, G-Money, Meka, and my dawg unborn seed!" he said then he started rapping to one of the Hot Boys song. "Set it off, set it off, fifty shots gonna set it off!"

***

Slim was sitting in his car talking to Boo on the phone while smoking a blunt.

"I know you going through a thing with your baby momma,

but you got some pussy in Off Spree apartments that's being neglected." Boo said into the phone in her sexiest voice.

"Oh yeah? Let me hear that pussy talk to me."

"Hold on." she said putting the phone by her pussy and started fingering herself so he could hear the smacking sound her wet pussy was making. "You hear that, baby? I know you hear my pussy calling you." she said when she got back on the phone.

"Yeah, I hear it." he replied massaging his dick. "Hold on baby, let me click over right quick. Somebody on my other line." Slim answered the other call. "Wussup Plat?" he asked after recognizing the number.

"Everything! Where you at?"

"Downtown. Why, wussup?"

"Them boy just shoot up the Bottom and your house!"

"What!? Hold on right quick my nigga." he switched back over to Boo. "Baby, let me call you back!"

"What's wrong? Everything alright?"

"I'll hit you back a'ight?" he switched back over to Plat before she could say or ask anything else. "Anybody get hurt?"

"D. Money was hit three times, Lil Kris was hit in the arm while coming through the cut, and Lil Corey was hit too. Bullets were hitting everything, cars and apartments. Is Lisa alright? She ain't been in that house init?"

"Nah she wasn't there and it's a good thing, too. Me and Butta duck off at Red's spot. I been outside, but I'm about to get them niggas and we coming to the Mount."

"Nah zeek, don't come nowhere near this bitch. It's too hot. Ain't nothing coming in or going out. I'm stuck around this bitch my damn self. We'll link up tomorrow."

"Bet it up. Be easy zeek."

After ending the call with Plat, Slim went into the house to tell Red and Butta about what happened on the Mount. Then he went upstairs to tell Lisa what happened to their house and her cousin Lil Kris. He told her not to worry because Lil Kris only got hit in the arm.

Later that night, Red, Tiny, Slim, and Lisa rode together to drop Butta off at one of his girlfriend's house out in an area known as Hub village in North Charleston. Then they all went over to Dave's Seafood restaurant in downtown Charleston to grab some dinner before heading back to the house.

While they were in the living eating their food, the news came on broadcasting the shooting that took place earlier in the 1251 apartments. Then they showed a scene of the shooting that happened on the Mount. They also flashed a clip of Slim and Lisa's house riddled with bullets. Seeing their house on the news made Slim and Red break down to Lisa and Tiny about the seriousness of the situation they were in. Lisa was already aware of what was going on, but she remained quiet and just listened.

Slim and Red told the ladies where the money and dope was located in case anything happened to them. They also filled them in on who were still indebted to them. After Red and Slim shared everything, they all sat in silence. Everyone caught up in their own thoughts. In the background, the news anchor could be heard reporting tha the police were now looking for the person who owned the home that had been shot up. They urged for the owner to come down to the North Charleston Police Department.

***

Bright and early the next morning, Slim entered Boo's apartment using his key. She was asleep in the room. He placed his belongings on her dresser and began undressing. He eased the sheets back and was surprised to see that she was already naked. The cool air made Boo shiver and turn over. She pulled her knees closer to her chest, but she never woke up.

The way her pussy lips poked out, from the fetal position that she was in, looked like two hamburger buns. Slim got down on his knees and moved his face to her pussy. He tilt his head to side and in one swift motion, he extended his tongue and licked her pussy from top to bottom. Boo tensed up and shifted, but she remained asleep.

Raising one of her leg, Slim watched as her pussy transformed from burger buns to a blossomed flower, exposing her cleanly shaved pussy to him. He used his tongue to spread her pussy lips open and then he began softly licking on her clit. He could taste her becoming wetter. Deep breaths and soft moans came from Boo's mouth, but she was still asleep. So, Slim used his right middle finger and index finger and slid it back and forth inside of her as he licked and sucked on her clit again. Boo stirred awake and gripped the sheets. When he hit her g-spot, she moaned and arched back.

"Coming…I'm coming." she moaned and began rotating her hips. She moaned and fucked Slim's fingers. "I'm coming Denzel, I'm coming."

Her legs started shaking as cum rolled down his fingers. When he replaced his fingers with his dick, Boo looked at him.

"You tired of my cat having your tongue?" she asked.

"I know your ass been woke. Calling me some fucking

Denzel. Denzel can't stroke this pussy like me." he replied.

"Tear this pussy up then." she moaned.

Slim was really feeling Boo. So, after they got through having sex, he told her a little bit about what was going on with him in the streets.

Boo held Slim and listened without saying a word. She was feeling Slim too, but she knew that he could never hers completely. She also wanted to tell him that she had missed her period, but after hearing what he had to say she decided to keep it to herself. Besides, it was too early to know for sure if she was pregnant or not.

CHAPTER 19

Lisa woke up from a bad dream and reached for Slim. She called his name, but Slim was nowhere in sight. She called his name a couple more times and still didn't get a response. So, she called out to Tiny and Red. They both came rushing into the room together thinking she was going through one of her episodes.

"I know where Trap them took me!" she said as Red and Tiny entered the room.

"Where Slim at?" Red asked.

"I don't know. He was gone when I woke up." she answered.

"Where they took you?" Tiny questioned.

"To some brick two story apartments on South Rhett. The apartments are on a curve."

"I know exactly where you're talking about." Red said rushing out the room to get his phone to call Slim. He came back in the room a couple minutes later to tell them Slim was on his way. Then he asked Lisa if she could remember the exact apartment that she was in.

"I'd have to show you." she replied.

"Tiny, go to your momma house and get her car. When Slim get here we all gonna ride on South Rhett so Lisa can point them boy spot out."

"Come ride with me." Tiny told Lisa.

When Tiny returned with her mother's car, Slim and Red were waiting outside on the porch smoking a blunt. It took them fifteen minutes to get from downtown to South Rhett. When they arrived at the area that Lisa mentioned, she pointed out the apartment that was located on the lower level.

"You sure that's the one?" Slim asked as Tiny rode pass.

"Yeah, I'm sure."

"A'ight. Shoot us back downtown. After y'all drop us off I want y'all to go by the hospital and check on D. Money."

"What about Lil Kris?" Lisa asked.

"He straight. I spoke with him this morning." Slim answered.

"What's D. Money real name?" Tiny asked.

"I know it." Lisa answered.

***

Lisa and Tiny came into the house about an hour and a half later from the hospital. Slim and Red were sitting on the couch drinking syrup and smoking a blunt. It was almost noon and they were waiting for the Channel 5 News to come on. Lisa and Tiny sat down and told them how D. Money was doing. Just as they began discussing the status of the other person who was shot, Slim cut them off.

"Hold on, we'll talk about that in a minute." Slim said cutting as he turned his attention to the TV. Anchor woman, Debi Chard, was on giving the breaking news.

"This is Debi Chard with your local Live 5 channel news. We are doing a follow up on a string of shootings that took place yesterday in the Charleston Farms community. Harv Jacob, can you tell the listeners what's going on?"

"Yes Debi, yesterday afternoon there was a shooting in the Marshview apartments off of Sumner avenue that left three individuals dead. The names of those victims are, Carlos Smalls, Bobby Hopkins, and Bryan Shaw. No suspects have been arrested. The North Charleston Police Department is looking for a man by the name of Tyron Green. He has been recognized as a person of interest. There was also another shooting that took place later that evening on Read street, where Daron Smith, Christopher Simmons, and Corey Knight were shot. Daron Smith suffered multiple gunshot wounds and is in the hospital recovering. Christopher Simmons and Corey Knight were released from the hospital last night. They have no suspects in this shooting either. Police are asking that anyone who may know anything about these crimes call Crime Stoppers at 843-554-1111. And also, if you see this man…"

An image of Tee Tee displayed on the screen.

"…don't hesitate to call Crime Stoppers or your local authority. Back to you, Debi."

***

Across town, at the spot, Tee Tee, Slugga and Trap were also watching the news.

"What tha fuck! Tee Tee, they got your face on the fucking news!" Trap said.

"Nigga you think I ain't got no eyes? I see that shit!" Tee Tee replied.

"Bruh, you hot as a fool." Slugga stated.

"You ain never lie. Damn!" Tee Tee said.

***

"Fuck! That goddamn Harv Jacob gets on my fucking nerves!" Detective Cummbee stated.

"Take it easy partner. They probably wasn't watching the news. We'll catch him." Detective Deckard replied.

"Even if he wasn't watching the news, somebody else was and probably done called him by now. I specifically told Harv not to mention Tyrone Green's name. Do you know how hard it's gonna be to catch him now that he knows we're looking for him? I could just strangle Harv!"

CHAPTER 20

Slim and Red were decked out in their hunting gear waiting on one of Red's peoples to come through with a stollo (stolen car). They both were high on pills and felt like they were on top of the world. While they sat on the porch smoking, two cars pulled up. The person Red was waiting for got out of one of the cars and approached them. Red paid the guy $150 for the car and he left. Slim and Red went inside and began strapping up. Red carried a Tech-9 and Slim carried two Glock 40's with extended clips. They gave Lisa and Tiny a kiss and told them that they would be back.

Before they left, Red ran back into the house to grab his Lil Boosie CD.

"We ain't riding to no Z-93 Jamz this time." he said, referring to the popular radio station, as he got back in the car. He inserted the CD into the player and skimmed until he got the song he wanted to hear. As Lil Boosie rapped the lyrics of his song, *Animosity*, Red and Slim drove off.

Halfway to their destination, Slim turned down the music.

"If we can get Trap out that mix alive, let's do it because I'ma let Lisa kill that nigga." Slim told Red.

"Alright," Red replied turning the music back up. He started rapping along with Boosie. "Animosity…smiling in my face you ain't my round…Animosity."

***

Trap left Tee Tee and Slugga in the apartment playing the Play Station 3, while he went to Burger King to get them something to eat. While he was in drive-thru, Slim and Red were turning into the South Rhett apartment complex parking lot.

As Trap was looking through his bag to make sure his order was right. Red and Slim were standing outside of the apartment door listening to Slugga and Tee Tee talk loudly while they played their game.

Slim silently counted to three with his fingers, then Red kicked the door in. Slugga was on his way to the bathroom when the door flew open. He got hit in the back three times before falling to the floor like a sack of potatoes. Tee Tee didn't stand a chance. He was caught off guard and never had a chance to reach for the pistol that was on the table in front of him.

When Trap pulled up in the parking lot, he could hear the gunshots and saw the flashes in the window. He grabbed his .380

from the passenger seat and got out the car. He waited for whoever was shooting in the apartment to come out.

Slim and Red went through the apartment, room to room, looking for Trap. After seeing that he wasn't there, they both said fuck it and figured they'd catch him later. As they were exiting the apartment, Slim was hit in the chest by two bullets. The impact threw him back into Red's arms. Red looked to see who had fired on them, the moment he saw Trap, a bullet slammed into his eye. Another one hit him in the shoulder. He fell to the ground with Slim still in his arms.

Trap walked up on Red and Slim and was about to shoot them again, but before he pulled the trigger, he heard somebody calling his name in the apartment. Not knowing if it were Tee Tee or Slugga, he rushed into the apartment calling their names. When he saw Tee Tee on the couch, he knew it wasn't him. Then he saw Slugga laying on the floor. Slugga called his name again.

"Slugga, you a'ight!" he asked leaning down by him.

"I can't feel my legs, bruh. Get me to the hospital. My back on fire." Slugga answered weakly.

Trap scooped him up and put him over his shoulder. He carried Slugga out of the apartment and to his car. After placing Slugga in the, car he ran back into the apartment and grabbed all the money and drugs that was stashed there. On the way out, he grabbed all the guns as well. He even took the guns Slim and Red had too and threw everything in the backseat. Trap jumped behind the wheel headed to the hospital. On the way there, he stopped by

Meka's mother house and told her to hold everything while he run his brother to the hospital. He dropped Slugga off at the emergency entrance of MUSC and left before anybody could ask him any questions.

***

"I think something happened to Slim and Red." Lisa said to Tiny.

"Why you say that?"

"I just called Slim's phone and it went straight to the voicemail. Plus, I just got that feeling that something ain't right."

"Red ain't answering either." Tiny said with her phone to her ear. She let the phone ring until the answer machine picked up. Then she tried again and still didn't get an answer.

"Come on, Tiny. Let's ride by them apartments." Lisa said getting off the couch.

When they made it to the South Rhett the apartments, police were everywhere. A few news vans were out there also, along with a couple of ambulances. The area was taped off with yellow crime scene tape. The nosy spectators lined the road trying see what was going on. Tiny pulled the car over and parked on the side of the road. Then she and Lisa jumped out and ran over to see what was happening.

Not asking anyone particular Lisa said, " What happen over there?"

258

A lady standing next to her said, "A couple people got killed over there."

Tiny took Lisa's hand and they both ran towards a police officer, that was standing off to the side.

"Officer! Officer!" Tiny and Lisa screamed. When they got the officer's attention, Tiny said, "I think two of those people over there are our baby daddies!"

"Calm down, ma'am. What are their names?" The officer asked.

"La'Mont Barr!" Lisa replied.

"Jasmond Welch!" Tiny echoed.

"Y'all stay right here. I'll be right back."

The officer walked off to talk to a few more officers standing near an ambulance. Minutes later, he came back and said they got both of them in the ambulance and are about to transport them to the hospital. He Lisa and Tiny know that they could ride with the ambulance if they wanted to. Tiny told him they drove and would follow the ambulance. Then they left.

Following behind the ambulances, Tiny and Lisa were both praying that Slim and Red were ok. When they got to St. Frances hospital in West Ashley, Slim and Red were both rushed to the back. Lisa and Tiny sat in the waiting room waiting to hear their fate.

Two hours later, a doctor came out to the waiting room and asked Lisa and Tiny if they there for La'Mont Barr. They both said yeah.

"I'm sorry to inform you that he didn't make it—"

Before the doctor could finish, Lisa started screaming. She tried to run into the operating room where Slim was, but the security guard stopped her.

Tiny felt sorry for Lisa and was bracing herself for the worst. They had to give Lisa something to calm her down and put her in a room where she could rest. Tiny was sitting by the bed when the same doctor stuck his head in the room and asked her to step out into the hall.

Tiny walked out into the hallway and said, "Just give it to me straight."

"Mr. Welch just came out of surgery. We were able to save his life, but we weren't able to save his left eye. I'll come back to let you know what room he's in when we assign him to one."

"Thank you." she said hugging him with tears rolling down her face. Then she headed back to Lisa's room.

***

"This is Harv Jacob reporting live from South Rhett avenue where in these apartments behind me three men were found shot multiple times. Police received a call about a shooting in the area and when they arrived they found three men shot in this apartment.

Two were rushed to the hospital and one was DOA. Police also have reports that a young man was dropped off at MUSC with multiple gunshot wounds. They believe he is connected to this shooting that took place tonight. Hold on a second...Police just released the name of the DOA victim, a Tyron Green. Yesterday we had Tyron Green on the news as a person of interest in a shooting that took place yesterday afternoon in Marshview apartments and tonight he was killed. North Charleston police believe all these shootings are related. Hold on a second...Sorry about that, but police have just confirmed that the young man that was dropped off to the hospital is the deceased victim's brother Tony Green. Authorities need your help locating this man—"

A photo of Trap was displayed on the screen.

"—his name is Travis Green, but he goes by the name Trap. As of right now, authorities just want to question him. Excuse me...this just came in, one of the victims that were transported to the hospital did not survive making this the fifth homicide in North Charleston in two days. If anyone has information on any of these shootings, police are asking that you contact Crime Stoppers at 843-554-1111 or contact your local authorities. You do not have to give your name."

Tiny used the remote on Lisa's bed to turn down the volume on the TV. Lisa was doing better, but she still couldn't believe Slim was dead.

"Lisa, you got to be strong. I'm sorry Slim is gone but you know he wouldn't want you to be carrying on like this." Tiny stated.

"I'm trying, Tiny. I'm trying. It ain't like he went to jail, and I can go see him or he'll come back home one day. My baby gone forever. He promised me he wouldn't leave me. What am I gonna tell Mann?" she cried again.

"And he ain't gonna leave you." Tiny said putting her arms around her. "He's gonna always be with you in spirit. Remember that. It's gonna take some time but Mann will understand as he gets older. Now, promise me you'll be strong for you and Mann."

"I promise but you also gotta make me a promise, too."

"You know I'm here for you and I always got your back. What I gotta promise?"

"Trap still alive and I'm not gonna let my baby lay in no grave while this nigga run round. I don't even want him to go to prison or nothing like that. I want him dead. He tore my whole family up. Word, you got to promise me you'll help me get my revenge. He need to feel the wrath of my animosity, our animosity. Are you with me on this?"

"Lisa, I don't even got to think twice on that. That's a major promise. His bitch ass dead and he don't even know it."

EPILOGUE

Two days after the shooting on South Rhett, Trap walked into the North Charleston Police Department with his lawyer to turn himself in. The following day, he was standing before a bond judge being charged with murder and assault and battery with intent to kill.

"I would like for my client to be granted a bond, Your Honor. He acted in self-defense." Trap's lawyer stated.

"Due to the nature of these crimes, I'm not at liberty to grant bond on a murder charge. That's up to the Supreme Courts, but I will set bond at 70,000 for the assault and battery with intent to kill. Next case." the Judge said after looking over Trap's files.

"Don't worry, Mr. Green, we'll get that bond in the preliminary hearing." Trap's lawyer assured him before an officer led Trap out the court room.

Two months later, Trap was walking out of the Charleston County Detention Center as a free man. His lawyer got all his charges dismissed on grounds of self-defense at his preliminary hearing.

***

When Boo heard the news about what happened to Slim and Red, she cried for hours. Tiny had called her to inform her and then she saw it again on the news. Once she was able to get herself together, she started cleaning her house in an attempt to take her mind off of everything. While she was cleaning her room, she noticed a brown bag on her dresser. She grabbed the bag and opened it up. Boo's eyes grew wide when she saw a bunch of money in rubber band stacks. As she dumped the money onto the bed, a letter fell out. She picked it up and start reading it.

Dear Boo Thing,

If you're reading this, then that means you're too damn nosy (smiles. I'm just joking. But seriously if you're reading this, I'm either in jail or dead.

This is just a lil token of my love for you. The rest is in my heart. I want you to know you're one of the realest bitches I ever met. And I don't mean that in a disrespectful way. If it wasn't for my BM, you would be my main gal. Even though our time together was short lived, I want you to know I did fall in love with you. Here's a lil something to help you along the way. Love you my Boo Thing.

- M$M Slim

When she got through counting the money it added up to fifty thousand.

With tears in her eyes, she whispered, "I will always love you Slim."

A month later, Boo was on the phone with Tiny telling her that she was pregnant and that it was Slim's baby. She told Tiny that she wanted to let Lisa know. Tiny told her that Lisa was with her and placed the phone on speaker.

When Boo had told Lisa that she was pregnant by Slim, Lisa didn't even trip.

All she said was, "I know I wasn't Slim's only gal and now Mann got a brother or a sister to play with."

Boo was expecting an argument but was glad that she and Lisa had an understanding.

After getting off the phone with Tiny and Lisa, Boo sat back on her bed and rubbed her stomach.

She smiled and said, "Slim, you're always gonna be in our hearts."

***

Red got out of the hospital a day before Slim's funeral. He still couldn't believe his main man was dead and he blamed himself because if it weren't for his animosity with Trap and his peoples, Slim would still be alive. He wished he could trade places with Slim.

A few days after Slim's funeral, Cool Hand and Key Key came to pick Red up and take him back to Tennessee for a few weeks while everything in Charleston calm down. Before he left, Red instructed Tiny to collect the money that was owed to him and Slim.

***

When Tiny and Lisa pulled on the Mount, people were still wearing R.I.P t-shirts with Slim's picture on it. After collecting the money, Tiny told everybody that she would get with them after she spoke with Red. She did that on purpose so they would know that all the money owed was expected with no exceptions. Red already had everything broken down before he left from the amount of money that was owed, to who it was due from, and what product each person was supposed to get. So, when Tiny and Lisa rolled back around a few hours later, they gave each person the dope as instructed.

For the first month and a half, Lisa stayed downtown at Tiny and Red's spot. When she finally went home to get her laundry, she couldn't believe how her house looked. Bullet holes were everywhere. While she was doing her laundry, she found a piece of paper in one of the pockets of her pants. It had Trap's number scribbled on it. Remembering how the number got in her pocket, she got on her cell phone and called Tiny to tell her what she found. At that moment, they devised a plan.

"Hello, is this Trap?" Lisa asked.

"Yeah, this me. Who this is?"

"This is Lisa."

"Girl, how the fuck you get my number? Better yet, what the fuck you calling me for?"

"You forgot? You gave me your number a while back. I just found it in one of pockets. I think you already know what I want."

"I feel ya. What you tryna get?"

"I was wondering if you could hook me and my girl up before we start getting sick. We'll do anything you want us to do."

"Who is this girl you got with you?"

"I don't think you know her. Her name Toya and she from downtown. Does it really matter who she is?"

"Where y'all at? And that bitch bet not be tear up."

"We at the Masters Inn on Rivers avenue behind the Churches."

Trap sucked on his teeth and said, "I know where the Masters Inn is at. Give me thirty minutes and y'all bitches better be naked when I get there."

***

When Trap got to the room, Lisa and Tiny were walking round butt naked. Trap was ready to get his freak on but before he could do that, he checked the room to make sure no one else was there besides them. After completing his search, he put a bundle of dope on the table and told Lisa and Tiny that they had to play before they got paid.

Lisa and Tiny already knew what they had to do because it was no limit to their revenge. Tiny laid on the bed and spread her legs open and Lisa put her head between Tiny's legs and started eating her pussy.

Ten minutes later, they were in the 69 position, while Trap sat in a chair across from them smoking a blunt and stroking his dick.

When he got through smoking his blunt, Lisa said, "Come get this pussy, nigga." She moved up on the bed and laid back on the pillows. She was really calling him a pussy nigga, but Trap didn't catch on.

Trap took a condom out his pocket and put it on. He got in the bed with Lisa, while Tiny sat in the chair he was just in, fingering herself. When Trap looked over and saw what Tiny was doing, he started fucking Lisa harder. Lisa's pussy was so wet and felt so good to him, that he made the mistake of closing his eyes. That's when he heard the click. When he opened his eyes, he was staring down the barrow of a snub nose .38. Before he could say anything, Tiny came up behind him and sliced his throat from ear to ear with a razor. When Trap grabbed at his throat, Lisa pulled the trigger sending a single bullet between his eyes.

Lisa let out a little scream when Trap's body fell forward on her. After she climb from under him, she and Tiny turned him over and Lisa took the condom off his semi hard dick and went to flush it. She came back into the room and to see that Tiny had cut Trap's dick off and was stuffing it in his mouth.

They both put on the gloves that they brought with them and started cleaning the room of any evidence that would've tied them to Trap's murder. After they left the room, and was turning on Rivers avenue, Tiny asked Lisa what took her so long to pull out the gun.

"Bitch, I ain't had no dick since Slim died. That shit been feeling too good. If you ain had did what you did, I probably would've let that nigga fuck until he bust a nut." she answered laughing. "I told you that nigga been gonna feel the wrath of our animosity."

"Yeah, you did." Tiny agreed.

Lisa's face became serious, "Now my baby can really rest in peace."

ABOUT THE AUTHOR

Jasmin Hudson was born and raised in Charleston, SC. He is a father, grandfather, and a newly published author. While incarcerated, Jasmin had to find a way to take his mind off of his current situation, so he picked up a pen and began writing. He had no idea that a few life experiences would turn into a novel.

His hope for his writing journey is that he can continue to create stories that gives a front row seat to real life issues. He is currently working on his next release.